A Candlelight Ecstasy Romance®

"PEG, YOU'RE ALWAYS CREATING SOME SCENE I CAN'T GET OUT OF WITHOUT PUTTING ON A PUBLIC SIDESHOW."

Stung, Peg reacted defensively. "Maybe," she said, "you're just too self-conscious. You embarrass too easily, David. You get mortified over things most people would take in stride."

"Is that so?" His voice rose. "Most people would take in stride the things you do? The things you put me through?"

"Well," she said, "I know I'm a bit careless sometimes, but—"

"Careless? You're a walking disaster! How many more surprises have you got up your sleeve? How many other secrets will I have to pull out of you before I know every infantile, misguided, humiliating—"

"None," Peg replied angrily. "I guess we're just not meant for each other."

CANDLELIGHT ECSTASY CLASSIC ROMANCES

MISCHIEF-MAKER

Molly Katz

A CANDLELIGHT ECSTASY ROMANCE®

Published by
Dell Publishing Co., Inc.
1 Dag Hammarskjold Plaza
New York, New York 10017

Dell ® TM 681510, Dell Publishing Co., Inc.

Candlelight Ecstasy Romance®, 1,203,540, is a registered trademark of Dell Publishing Co., Inc., New York, New York.

ISBN: 0-440-15572-X

Printed in the United States of America

May 1987

10 9 8 7 6 5 4 3 2 1

WFH

For the real Peg Bailey,
my beloved and lovely friend

And for the real Shirley Hewitt,
who is very much missed.

To Our Readers:

We have been delighted with your enthusiastic response to Candlelight Ecstasy Romances®, and we thank you for the interest you have shown in this exciting series.

In the upcoming months we will continue to present the distinctive sensuous love stories you have come to expect only from Ecstasy. We look forward to bringing you many more books from your favorite authors and also the very finest work from new authors of contemporary romantic fiction.

As always, we are striving to present the unique, absorbing love stories that you enjoy most—books that are more than ordinary romance. Your suggestions and comments are always welcome. Please write to us at the address below.

Sincerely,

The Editors
Candlelight Romances
1 Dag Hammarskjold Plaza
New York, New York 10017

MISCHIEF-MAKER

CHAPTER ONE

He took off his charcoal suit jacket and hung it over the back of the small room's one chair. He hooked his finger around his tie knot, loosened it, and pulled the tie off. Next he unbuttoned his pale blue shirt, removed it, and draped it over the jacket. Then he took his T-shirt off.

Peg looked at the brawny ridges along his stomach. A patch of very black hair, darker than the brown side-brushed hair on his head, divided his thick pectoral muscles. His arms showed the heavy cords of a man who worked out. They swelled enticingly as he undressed.

A jittery excitement began to bubble inside her.

He sat down and untied one gleaming black wingtip, pulled it apart to loosen the laces, and slipped it off. Then he placed the other one next to it, took off his black socks, and put them on the shoes. Peg wasn't sure why he was taking off his socks, never mind his shirt, but she was too fascinated to puzzle over it.

She watched as he stood, opened his belt, unzipped his pants, and got out of them. His thighs, thickly covered with hair, were solid blocks of virility. In fact, his legs were handsome all the way down, the thighs narrowing to well-shaped knees and strong calves.

As well as she knew her phone number, Peg knew she should have stopped him. She could get into a lot of trouble. It wouldn't have been hard to speak up right at the start, instead of letting him go this far. Now she was really nervous, but it was too late; the whole business was past the point of no return. She had no choice but to stay where she was and watch as he took off everything, revealing his body limb by gorgeous limb.

Everything but his shorts, anyway. The boxer briefs fit trimly, hinting at an appealingly rounded rear. Standing there in them, he could have been posing for a designer-underwear ad.

Her heart was going faster and faster. She was shocked at herself, boldly looking on while a man stripped almost bare only feet from her, and her guilt was growing sharper every second as she felt the familiar chagrin of knowing she should be handling something more sensibly. But it was so hard to be sensible with temptation like this! Not only was the guy's build incredible; he'd been a dream before he took a stitch off, with his strong squarish face and gray eyes that looked calm and dynamic at once. He had a wide mouth—she loved that in a man—and though his nose was a little big, it fit with his other features. His hair looked as if he paid by the strand to have it barbered, and his hands . . . well, they were the best, large and wide, with strong-looking fingers.

He probably had a beautiful back, too, and she'd

find out any second, as soon as he turned to get one of the bathing suits that hung on the wall hook.

But he wasn't doing that. He was holding the waistband of his shorts. He was going to take them off.

Peg's eyes went wide and then closed in self-conscious confusion. Her hands were sweating. Who would have thought he'd take his *shorts* off? Hadn't he seen the—

Of course not, she realized. How likely was he to have spotted the discreet little notices in the Resort Wear department that asked you to wear undergarments to try on swimsuits . . . when he'd completely missed the big sign next to the mirror he was looking at that said, These ladies' fitting rooms monitored by female security personnel?

He was actually doing it now, getting out of his shorts. Peg gasped, and then clapped her hand over her mouth to stifle any further sound.

She watched with a hammering pulse as he tried on a maroon bathing suit with a navy side stripe, turned to view himself from all angles, and then took it off. He was even more fantastic-looking nude, sexier than the models in her roommate's *Playgirl* calendar. The natural, easy way he moved around the dressing room, thinking himself totally alone, only heightened the effect.

He tried on the other one, a blue-and-green paisley. It was a little shorter and tighter, and Peg knew even before he stepped out of it and clipped it back on the hanger that he'd take the maroon.

He put his shorts back on and started to dress. The store detectives' enclosure—the coop—where

Peg stood riveted to one of the two-way mirrors was stuffy and warm, but she couldn't blame her damp blouse on that alone. Her head was swimming with excitement, disbelief, guilt—

—and panic, suddenly, as she realized that however he'd made the mistake of wandering in here without anyone seeing, the man still had to get *out*. Betty Henry was the fitting room checker this afternoon; she must have been on a quick trip to the water fountain when he came in. A beetle couldn't walk out past Betty without a thorough inspection; there wasn't much chance she'd fail to notice that someone was the wrong sex.

Peg rubbed her eyes and tried to think. What was she going to do? She was responsible for fitting room security when she was in here; if Betty mentioned to Mr. Burgholtz that a man had gotten in, her boss would be on her back yet again.

She wished she'd paid attention to her better judgment in the first place. She should have chased the man right out as soon as she saw him, instead of standing there like a—a—Peeping Thomasina.

He was putting on his tie now, crossing the ends to make the knot. He leaned close to the mirror to loop the top through, so near that they were practically kissing. Peg's pulse began to skitter again. Though heavy glass separated them, she could almost feel his warm breath on her face. It was as if she could extend her hand just inches and touch his broad jaw with its tickle of whiskers . . . and he could stroke her golden brown curls, caress with a finger the usually upturned mouth that was solemn now.

She made herself turn from the mirror-window and leave the coop.

She went out to Betty, wondering wildly what she could do to distract the woman.

"Peg!" Betty said. "What's wrong?"

"Wrong?" Peg croaked.

"You look all upset, dear. Is there a security problem? Do you need help?"

"Yes," Peg said, grateful for the leading question. "Would you see if you can find a woman for me? There are two I need to locate, and they went separate ways," she went on, improvising as she talked. "I'll follow the one who went into Resort Wear, and you can look in the other direction. In—uh—"

"Coats?"

"Coats! Yes!" Peg said. The department was way across the floor. "Hurry!"

"What does she look like?" Betty asked, poised to run.

"She's, um, black. No, white. I mean," Peg rushed on as Betty looked oddly at her, "her dress is black. And white. Look for someone in a black-and-white dress."

The short dark-haired woman hurried away, and Peg slumped against the wall. Then she heard a door squeak; the man was coming out. She darted behind a mirrored pillar and watched as he strolled unconcernedly out of the fitting room in a gray cashmere overcoat, carrying the maroon swimsuit.

Her beeper sounded, its soft blips making her jump. She went back into the empty fitting room and took her two-way radio out of her handbag.

"Yes?" she whispered into it.

15

"Bailey?" Mr. Burgholtz said. "Go to the street door. Woman in her thirties, peroxide blond, red coat. Extra blouse in her shopping bag."

Fantasy time was over. Peg put the radio away and hurried down to the main entrance of the uncrowded store. She saw a flash of red through the door and went out. The woman was right there.

"Excuse me," she said. "My name is Miss Bailey. I'm a store detective. Let me see your shopping bag, please."

The woman's pale, expertly penciled eyebrows rose. She pushed a wheat-colored strand of hair behind her ear. She was closer to fifty than thirty, Peg guessed, but she wore the years beautifully. Her lovely features were marred only by her arrogant frown.

"Who," the woman asked, holding the gold-and-silver Smith-Clove shopping bag slightly behind her, "do you think you are?"

"As I told you," Peg said, reaching for the bag, "I'm a store detective. I have reason to suspect you're carrying merchandise you didn't pay for."

Their voices were low, and the few customers passing by barely glanced their way. Peg didn't want to make a scene, but if the woman kept shifting the bag away as she was doing, she'd have no choice.

"I can sue you, you know." The woman's fine mouth curled. "You shouldn't harass a good customer. Get out of my way, if you don't mind. I'm in a hurry."

Moving quickly, Peg grabbed the bag's handle. She gave it a good yank, but the woman held on.

"What's the problem here?" she heard a man say behind her. Still clutching the bag, she turned—and dropped it. The man from the fitting room stood there.

"Can I help?" he asked the blond woman.

"Oh, yes, please," she said.

"No, thank you," Peg said at the same time.

The woman turned suddenly winsome eyes on the man. Her vicious expression had gone sweetly helpless in a blink. Peg was chagrined to note the man's response. He was looking down at her with protective concern.

"This person is confusing me with someone else," the woman said. "I'd be glad to help if I could, but since it's a mistake, and I *am* in a hurry, there's nothing I—"

"Excuse us," Peg told the man. "This is no mistake. It's a confidential security matter."

Before either of them could say anything else, Peg made another grab for the shopping bag and got it. Turning away fast, out of reach, she pulled a peach-colored blouse out from under some properly bagged purchases.

"That's mine!" the woman cried. "Give it back!"

The man took the bag and the blouse from Peg with such confident force that if she hadn't let go, both would have been torn. He held the blouse up to look at it.

"You bought this?" he asked the woman.

"Yes," she said, the picture of bruised dignity. "And I *must* be going." She reached to take the blouse from him. "Thank you for your help."

"Just a second," he said. He held up a sleeve to

show a red splotch on the peach silk. "This is stained. You don't want to pay good money for a damaged blouse. I suggest you go back in and exchange it."

"She's going back in," Peg said, "but not to make an exchange." She stared him smack in his chilly gray eyes. "She's coming down to the security office."

He stared right back. "The lady seems very sure that this is a mistake. You're hassling her for nothing. Look at her." He gestured at the blonde, her exquisitely tailored red coat, her impeccable hair and makeup. "Does this look like someone who needs to steal?"

"They usually don't look like people who need to steal," Peg answered tightly.

"Oh, is that right?" he challenged. "Is that what they teach you in whatever three-week training program you take for this job?"

She didn't have to defend herself against such condescending insults from a meddler. "I'll tell you again," she said. "This is a security problem. Leave us—"

"What it is," he said indignantly, "is a flagrant case of disrespect for your clientele. Smith-Clove is an exclusive store that attracts the highest-quality shopper, and people who come here should not have to put up with rude interference from an officious nuisance like you." He shook his finger at her. She was mad enough to bite it. "Learn some courtesy. Learn how to treat the Smith-Clove customer, or you're going to lose a lot of them."

"What's taking so long, Bailey? I've been waiting

for you downstairs," Peg heard Hugh Burgholtz say behind her. "Oh, it's a couple? Didn't realize that." He snatched the blouse.

The man in gray was apparently too surprised by Hugh Burgholtz's comment to hold on to it.

"*Couple?*" he said. "You think I—"

"He was just passing by. And butting in," Peg told her boss, fighting the urge to use stronger words. "He has nothing to do with the blouse."

"What's this on it?" Burgholtz demanded, scowling as he peered at the sleeve. Side-combed strands of black hair latticed a bald spot on top of his head. "Now they're lifting soiled merchandise? Kinky."

"Who the hell are you?" the man in the gray coat asked.

Mr. Burgholtz raised his head slowly. "I'm the security director of the store. That's who the hell I am. As for who the hell *you* are, I don't care. Beat it."

He went to take the blouse back. "Don't you talk to—"

"Leave that alone!" Peg said, pushing his hand away.

The man looked at his shirt cuff. The blue cotton was smudged with red.

"What the— Come here," the man said, grabbing Peg's hand. He turned it over to see the palm. There was red on it.

"What's that? Lipstick, it looks like."

Peg pulled her hand away, resisted the impulse to clap it over her mouth, and instantly realized what had happened. That habit didn't usually cause trouble, since she wore pale lipstick; but she'd tried on a screaming-red gloss at one of the cosmetic counters during her lunch break. When she'd covered her mouth to stifle her gasp in the dressing room . . .

"God, Bailey," her boss said disgustedly. He held up the blouse. "This is your work too? You're incredible."

Peg clenched her teeth but kept quiet. Later she'd have another talk with him about reprimanding her in public, but for now she'd only be lowering herself to his level of unprofessionalism by speaking out.

The man in the elegant gray coat turned to the blond woman. "She admits she got your blouse dirty. Return it," he urged. "They should give you a new one free, for all the trouble they're causing you."

"Oh," she said with a dismissive gesture, "I'm sick of this. Keep the stupid thing. I'll have my account credited for—"

"No way," Hugh Burgholtz said, taking her elbow. "We're going downstairs."

She rolled her eyes but didn't protest further. The man said, "If you can't straighten this out, call me— I'm your witness. Here's my card."

Peg glanced at it. She caught only his name and firm before the woman took it and went inside with the security director. Peg watched David Robertson walk off with his own shopping bag, the contents of which she knew so well.

It was hard to believe the stuffy, self-important jerk was the same man whose tantalizing—albeit unintentional—performance she'd watched from just inches away. Striding down the sidewalk, his open coat blowing a bit in the January wind, he looked like every pompous, boring businessman she saw on the streets of Hartford. No sensitivity, no sparkle, no fun—just a rat in the rat race.

Well, she should have known. Beautiful biceps or not, only a man with no imagination has to take off *everything* to try on a bathing suit.

"I found her," Betty Henry said between breaths. "Where—have you been? I've been looking all over."

"Found who?" Peg asked.

"The woman in—the black-and-white dress. Boy! I surely don't—have the wind I used to." She leaned against a pillar near the escalator. "She's upstairs with—"

"Betty, I'm sorry, but—*what* woman in the black-and-white dress?"

Betty stared at her. "Are you sure you're all right, hon? The one you told me to look for. In Coats. She's upstairs. Darcy Carter is holding her so I could come and find you."

"Oh, Lord," Peg said, remembering.

"She's awful angry. Hissing like a snake. Of course, she says it's all a mistake. Incredible how every last one of them says that."

"Incredible," Peg said.

"Did you catch the one you wanted?"

"Yes. I mean, no. Well, yes, we have a woman, but —look," Peg said, "could you tell Darcy something for me?"

"But," Betty asked, her pleasant face bewildered, "aren't you going over there now?"

21

"I can't. I'd like to, but I have to, um . . ."

"Well, hon, *I* have to get back to the fitting rooms. We haven't been busy, but you never know when someone's going to come in, do you?"

"No," Peg said fervently.

"Goodness. With both of us gone, the rooms are wide open. I'd better hurry." She turned toward the escalator.

Peg said, "Tell you what. I'll run back there and cover things for both of us. You take a detour past Coats and give Darcy my message." She stepped onto the moving stairs with Betty.

"What's the message?"

"Tell her to let the woman go."

Betty gaped at her.

"I'm sorry, but it *was* a mistake." They reached the second floor. The older woman started to talk, but Peg said, "I'll explain later—we don't want to leave the fitting rooms open," and quickly walked off.

She'd think of some way to square things with Betty and Darcy, but she just hadn't wanted to deal with still another outraged customer—especially an outraged customer who was *right*.

She went into the coop. All the fitting rooms were empty. She glanced at the one she'd watched David Robertson do his unwitting striptease in. She closed her eyes in remembered pleasure and in regret— regret that she'd ended up meeting the man. How disappointing to find out what a condescending stuffed shirt he was. She should never have let him stay in the dressing room—but since she had, she'd rather have carried away only the dreamlike fantasy-memory of a handsome anonymous body.

22

CHAPTER TWO

Peg said, "Tell me you don't mean it."

"I didn't think you'd be upset," Diane said.

"But I'll miss you."

Peg pushed a clump of wet hair away from her face and brushed pearly powder onto one high cheekbone. Diane sprayed on cologne, put the bottle back on the shelf, and left the bathroom.

"When are you moving?" Peg shouted after her.

"The twenty-eighth."

"Of *January?* That's so soon!"

"Come on, Peg. Grown women can survive without roommates."

"I can 'survive' without jelly doughnuts," Peg grumbled, coming into the bedroom, "but I don't want to. You and I have so much fun. I wish you'd stay."

Diane leaned toward the dresser mirror to put on a crystal earring that glowed against her short auburn hair. "These wake up the old black dress, don't they? Listen, the listing just opened up. The realtor said I had to move fast. You know how badly I want a beach cottage. I grabbed it." She turned and smiled. "I'll miss you, too, though." She was quiet while she put on the other earring. "I thought you wouldn't want to room with *me* much longer. I was getting the impression you and Ron would make it permanent soon."

Peg scowled. "If Ron could make *anything* permanent."

Diane eyed her with raised brows.

"You know how he is," Peg went on. "If I hear him say one more time that we're going to play it by ear, I'll throw up."

"Your relationship—"

"I don't mean our relationship. It was never that deep. But a movie, anything—the man is positively allergic to committing himself." She squeezed blue gel from a tube onto her palm and rubbed it into her hair. "He doesn't even have a lease on his apartment. He pays month by month."

"You told me."

"If he could write in disappearing ink and get away with it, he would. Are you going to take that lipstick to work with you?"

"I can leave it. Here."

"Thanks."

Diane studied her. "Awful lot of trouble for a day off. Are you going somewhere in particular?"

"Sort of," Peg said. The words were distorted as she spoke without moving her mouth.

"But if Ron—"

"Not with Ron." It sounded like "nuh wih Won." She recapped the lipstick. "I've had enough of Ron, I think."

"So," Diane persisted, "what are you getting so nicely done up for?"

"I might . . . meet someone."

Diane laughed. "I *am* going to miss you. You're cooking up one of your whoppers, aren't you?"

Peg pushed her collar-length hair around with her fingers, hoping she'd used enough gel to make it dry in curls. With the weather so bitingly cold and dry, it tended to go lank.

"Don't give me that innocent look," Diane said. "What are you planning?"

"Why do you think I—"

"Oh, Peg," she said. "Who knows your capers better than I do? Let's see, there was the time you took fishing lessons. You didn't like the instructor, so you put a whole container of earthworms in his—"

"I remember," Peg said shortly.

"And the plumber? The one you wanted to go out with? To get him here on a Saturday night, you deliberately unscrewed the—"

"Diane—"

"Well, can you understand why I know the warning signs by now? A person can't live with you for three years and not see when all hell is about to break loose. What is it this time? A joke? A man? Something else?" She left the room and went to the coat closet.

Peg followed her. "Where's my green sweater?"

"I don't know. Green sweater, huh? It must be a man. You don't need a fit like that for earthworms."

"Seriously, where is it?"

"You wore it last."

"I did?"

Diane put on her coat and buttoned it. "Definitely. About two weeks ago."

"Well, I've looked everywhere," Peg said. "The closet, the laundry, your laundry—"

"Did you look in your sweater drawer?"

"No." Peg went back into the bedroom. "Oh, good. It's here. See? You can't move. What will I do without you?"

But Diane had already said good-bye and left for work.

She pulled on the turtleneck carefully, so as not to muss her hair or makeup, then stepped into her new ivory wool skirt and went to the full-length mirror on the bathroom door. She looked at herself from the back and sides as well as the front. She unzipped the skirt and tucked the sweater in. That was better; the knit helped soften her thinness, and her bust looked almost respectable.

She went around the room putting things away, thinking about her plan. She was nervous, but excited. It just might work.

The building had no lot, but Peg had left home way before noon in case of such a problem, and she found a parking space that was close enough so she could stay in the car and watch the entrance. She wouldn't have lasted long if she'd had to wait outdoors. The sun was out, but the temperature was only nineteen degrees, and what the radio referred to as breezy described a wind that, in Peg's opinion, could have knocked over a mid-size Ford.

Plus, she was wearing her highest-heeled sexy ankle-straps, and they had open toes.

It hadn't occurred to her until she was walking out the door that when she "ran into" David Robertson, she'd have her coat on; he might never see the outfit she'd chosen so painstakingly if she couldn't inspire him to invite her to lunch. She'd decided that if her coat and shoes were going to be all he saw at first, the shoes had better be good.

Twelve o'clock came, and people began to leave the office buildings on the street. Peg kept watch for David, but she didn't expect to see him this early. He'd been shopping for his swimsuit at two, so unless she was wrong, he was a late luncher.

The sun warmed the car through the windshield. She watched the noontime parade of men and women in smart-looking outerwear, some with hats, many with briefcases. She wished she'd gotten around to replacing her yellow coat. She'd loved it when she bought it three years ago, but it was shapeless and ratty now from constant wear. She'd meant to get a new coat for weeks; she shouldn't have put that off. But who would have thought she'd suddenly need to look fabulous for an outdoor encounter?

For that matter, who would have thought she'd ever want to look fabulous for David Robertson?

That crazy experience in the dressing room two weeks ago was one of the wildest things that had ever happened to her. Then her dream-god had ruined it by appearing on earth—clothed, pompous, and nasty.

But he'd appeared again . . . and again and again. In her dreams and in her thoughts. With every visitation the image shifted a little; he became easier, nicer, more fun, and less *dressed*. David the Naked was replacing David the Dull. Her fantasy mind was busily erasing the second meeting and enhancing the first.

She'd begun thinking she wanted to see him again.

Of course, the whole thing was being helped along, in a backward way, by Ron. Their on-and-off dating had become more off as Peg tired of his irresponsible side. Oh, he was enjoyable to be with and always ready for a fun escapade—but that wore thin when the chocolate coating was all there was.

She loved a good time herself; she'd be the first to say so. But good times weren't everything.

The more she thought about David Robertson, the more the very things that had turned her off began to look interesting. He'd been rude, but she sensed that wasn't his usual way. He was stuffy . . . but it would be a nice change to date someone who didn't pay for a can of coffee with a postdated check —that is, if he wanted to go out with *her*. And she planned to do her best to make him want to.

Her watch said one, then one fifteen. The car was still warm, but the heat didn't reach under the dashboard, and her feet were like ice.

Maybe she should have checked the phone book to see whether Valley Realty had other branches. This was the only office she knew of, but that didn't mean it was the only one in existence.

One thirty.

An awful thought struck her. For heaven's sake. She was an airhead. She'd forgotten that real estate people don't spend regular hours in their offices. She'd probably been sitting here all this time for nothing. She should have thought of some other

28

way to meet him. A phone ruse, maybe. She was a trained detective. She could certainly have come up with—

There he was, leaving the building. Not only that, he was walking fast. Not only *that*, he was walking fast in the other direction, away from her.

She got out quickly, shut the door, took three steps, and found herself sitting on the sidewalk. The four-inch heels she wasn't used to, combined with her numb toes, had made her lose her balance.

People stopped to help her up. A man took her arm and pulled her to her feet; a woman tried to brush the gray off her coat, unaware that the gray-ness was permanent. Someone handed her back her car keys.

Peg thanked them all and rushed off as fast as she could in the sandals. Every time she wore them, she remembered why she never did. They were a lovely coffee-with-cream color, but they made her feel like she was walking on pogo sticks.

She hurried along the sidewalk, searching for David's glossy brown hair and gray cashmere coat. The tall buildings intensified the wind; the face-framing curls she'd arranged with such care were gone, and tears streaked her blush.

She spotted him standing with one foot off the curb, waiting for a light to change. She walked faster. When she reached him, she stepped off the curb, too, and turned as if checking for traffic.

"Oh," she said as brightly as possible, nearly out of breath. "It's you! Well, hello—" She broke off as she saw she was greeting a brown-haired man in a gray cashmere coat who was at least fifty.

She could feel his perplexed stare as she raced across the street, trying to watch her footing and the people around her at the same time. Gray coat, bald . . . gray coat, too short . . .

Suddenly there he was, half a block ahead, walking into a delicatessen.

Peg started to hurry toward him, then slowed as she realized she could take her time now; he probably wasn't stopping there just for a book of matches. This was lucky. How much easier to "bump into" him in a nice warm deli than to meet him on the Siberian sidewalk, trying to look cheerily pretty while willing her toes not to drop off.

Peg ducked into a doorway next to the deli. Using a display window for a mirror, she wiped her wet eyes and smoothed her blush as best she could. She fluffed her hair, trying to restore the curly tumble, but it was no use; the gel that had held the curls in place was obeying the wind's influence instead, and her spirals were now pointy spikes. She poked and pulled, but there was no curl left at all. She gave up, took a brush from her purse, and smoothed it all down. Now it was straight and blah, but at least it wasn't frightening.

She went into the deli. David Robertson was sitting at the counter with a sandwich in front of him. Her fairy godmother, she noted delightedly, was on duty: there were only two empty seats, and one was next to him.

Her heart thudding, she went over and sat. He didn't look in her direction.

A wave from her fairy godmother's wand: the menu was on the wall to her right. David Robertson sat to her right. Which meant that when she looked over to see the menu, it seemed easy and natural for her to say:

"Well, hello there. Remember me?"

He turned to her. She was totally unprepared for the effect he had on her. A magnetic aura seemed to flow from him. The smoothly muscled flesh fairly glowed beneath his clothes, the memory causing an X-ray sensation so strong that she had to close her eyes for a moment.

And his voice—she hadn't noticed his voice before, probably because the first encounter had been a silent movie, and in the second, she'd been too mad. But now she felt a flutter inside at the golden richness, the depth and resonance, when he said:

"No."

She swallowed in hurt disappointment. "It was two weeks ago," she said. "At Smith-Clove. When you, uh . . ." She made herself stop babbling. She had to watch it; she'd almost mentioned the fitting rooms. He was rattling her so, she'd wreck everything if she didn't throw her mind into overdrive, and fast.

"I'm Peg Bailey," she began again. "I'm the store detective who was questioning a shoplifter when you—stopped to help."

"Oh," he said, and went back to his sandwich.

Peg clenched her hands and pretended to study the menu on the wall. This was more fun than stepping on a hornets' nest—but not by much. What confidence she had was ebbing. The man's attitude was an ice bath.

She hadn't gone to all this bother just to be frozen

out—but if he was only going to toss her single syllables, she was out of options.

"You look different from the first time I saw you," he said, turning back to her.

Not as different as you do from the first time I saw *you*, she thought, and clapped her hand over her mouth even though she hadn't spoken aloud. As she now did automatically, she checked her palm and then cleaned it off.

"Oh, right. I remember all of it now," he said. "The dry cleaner couldn't get the lipstick off my shirt." He glared accusingly at her.

Somebody must have chloroformed her fairy godmother.

"Yes, miss?" a waiter said. "What would you like?"

"Uh . . ." Her mind had stopped working completely. "That," she said, pointing to David Robertson's sandwich.

"And?"

"Pardon?" she asked.

"Something to drink? Coffee? Soda?"

"No, thank you." The way things were going, she didn't trust herself with liquid.

She glanced toward the door and noticed that there was a rack; she could have ditched her coat there when she came in and greeted him the way she'd planned all morning, in her nice green sweater tucked in just so. Instead she was sitting on the stool with the thing brushing the floor, getting grimier by the minute.

"I think," she said as coolly as she could, "I'll go

hang up my coat." She went to the rack and came back. Her sandwich had come.

"You didn't have your hair that way," David Robertson said in his delicious voice. "It was curly two weeks ago, wasn't it?"

It was curly fifteen minutes ago, Peg thought, but she said, "I like to wear it all different ways." Maybe that would take the sting out of the impression her coat had made. She always admired women who had the fashion sense to change their hairstyles often.

"You ought to go back to the other way," he said.

She felt a sharp point of hurt. This was turning out to be a lot harder than she'd expected. He clearly didn't find her the least bit attractive.

Should she just finish her lunch and give up? How much could her ego take? It was fine to give a man a little push if you had to, but she was beginning to think a bulldozer couldn't move David Robertson in her direction.

She picked up her sandwich and took a bite. Well, she'd invested half a day and risked frostbite, a broken ankle, and pneumonia—she might as well give it a few more minutes. If she concentrated really hard on being serene and poised and elegant . . . looked meaningfully into his eyes . . . chatted a little, tried for a tantalizing "mystery woman" effect. . . .

"Ugh!" she yelled suddenly, involuntarily. It was all she could do not to be sick. Whatever was in her sandwich was horrible, the texture thick and wet and bumpy. "What *is* this?"

Now she had David Robertson's full attention—

and everyone else's. The entire population of the restaurant was looking her way.

"Shh. It's what you ordered—chopped chicken liver," he said, glancing around uncomfortably.

Peg dropped the sandwich as though he'd announced it was radioactive.

"This is *liver?*" she demanded. "In a *sandwich?*"

"You ordered it," he said again. He turned on his stool to face her. "What's the matter? Didn't you— Here, drink this," he told her, pressing his mug of coffee into her hands when he saw her face still wrinkled with disgust. "Didn't you know what my sandwich was? I thought that was why you asked for one."

She gulped the coffee gratefully, but when she put the empty cup down, her mouth was still a swamp. She'd just discovered that there was something worse than the taste of liver. It was the taste of liver combined with coffee. She looked around for a glass of water, saw one in front of the person to her left, took it, and drank it.

When that glass was empty she could finally say "Sorry" to the nonplussed woman she'd taken it from. She said it again to David Robertson, who was watching her with the same expression.

Peg said, "I have to be going." She fished through her big purse for her wallet. She couldn't wait to get out of here. Of all times not to be able to find her money. Maybe the deli would accept her wristwatch as payment.

"No way," he said firmly.

She looked up. "Excuse me?"

"You can't leave," he said. His gray eyes were determined; his lips were as wide and lush as she remembered from the fitting room. "Not without an explanation."

"An explanation," Peg echoed, horror filling her. How had he figured out that this was all a setup? How could she endure the humiliation of—

"You bet. Why does someone look at my sandwich, order the same thing, and then practically die in front of me?"

She was so relieved to find he didn't know why she was here that she answered with the truth.

"I didn't know what kind of sandwich it was."

"Why did you order it, then?"

Peg looked down at her lap. "I was flustered."

"Why?" he persisted.

She shrugged. Her wits, usually quick to supply any invention needed, seemed to be on vacation. She raised her eyes and shrugged again.

He didn't seem the sort who was conscious of his attractiveness, so something in her face must have revealed the answer. As Peg watched with surprise, he went cranberry red.

Now she felt worse than ever. To have something to do, she picked up the cup she'd emptied and gave it to the passing waiter.

"Could we have more coffee, please?" she asked.

It was only when the filled cup was back and she was handing it to David that she saw the lipstick on the rim. It was pale apricot rather than bordello scarlet; maybe he wouldn't mind this time.

"Sorry about the lipstick," she said.

"Yeah," he said. "That was my favorite shirt."

"No. The cup."

"Oh." He peered at it. "No problem. I don't have to wear it."

He lifted the cup and drank. Peg saw his big shoulder and upper arm outlined beneath his jacket, and warmth flooded her as the image of his nakedness came crashing into her thoughts.

"Listen," she said impulsively, "why don't *I* clean your shirt?"

He turned to her. "You?"

"Yes, me. I'm not just a pretty face, you know."

He grinned, his first real grin. It made his handsome face even more attractive. "You're not?" he asked softly, banteringly.

The syrup-smoothness of his voice made her tremble. "I happen to be good at taking spots out."

"Oh," he said with new respect. "Well, sure, if you don't mind." He finished his coffee. He smiled at her again. "Your place or mine?"

"Uh, mine," she said, for no better reason than that it was the first word to leave her mouth. "When would be convenient for you?"

"Well," he said, his grin widening, "right now I have to get back to the office."

"Oh! I didn't mean—"

"I know you didn't. I was teasing. I'll be out of town this weekend, but how about next Friday night? Let me take you to dinner afterward. I promise I'll pick a place that has no liver."

The waiter put his check on the counter.

"Gee," Peg said. "That would . . . Sure." She smiled. "I'd like to. Thank you." She turned to the waiter. "Can I have my check, please?"

"You wanted separate checks?" the waiter asked. "Yours is on his."

"Oh, but—"

"Never mind," David Robertson said. "It's the least I can do." He took another bill out of his wallet. "Give me your address. I'll be there at seven."

"Right," Peg said. She pawed through her purse again for a pen. She couldn't find one. She tried all the places they usually hid, but no luck. She was so excited over her success, even with the multiple disasters, that her hands were shaking.

She heard a click. David Robertson was holding out a pen. She took it and grabbed a napkin and started to write on it. Patiently he took away the napkin and handed her a small leather-bound notebook, open to a clean page. She wrote her address and gave his things back.

"A week from Friday at seven," she said as he got up. "See you then."

He said, "Don't you want to know my name?"

"I kn-I—" She swallowed. That had been close. "Yes. I *need* to know your name. What is it?"

"David Robertson." Not Dave. Somehow she'd known. "Take it easy."

She watched him get his coat, put it on, and leave, her mind making flash pictures—David dressed, David not dressed, David dressed, David not dressed. . . .

"You?" her mother said.

"Well," Peg said crossly, "I'm not a complete incompetent, you know."

"Of course not," she said soothingly. "Hold on, will you, dear? There's someone at the door."

She was back in a minute. "The paper boy. Why do people always ring the bell when I'm on long distance? Sorry. Where were we?"

"You were reassuring me that I'm not a complete incompetent," Peg said.

"Well, naturally you're not. It's just that I've never known you to be particularly interested in things like spot cleaning."

"I'm not, really. I have to get a stain out of a shirt, and I wanted your advice."

"Certainly. My advice is to take it to a dry cleaner."

"Oh," Peg said. "That's already been done."

"Then don't waste your time any further," Ellen Bailey said briskly. "Throw the thing out."

"I can't do that."

"Why not?"

"Well," Peg said, starting to feel panicky, "it's, um, a favorite."

"That's a shame. What's the stain?"

"Lipstick."

Her mother was silent for a minute. "Peg," she said, "this isn't one of your scrapes I'd prefer not to know about, is it?"

"Why do you ask? All I did—"

"A mother's instinct. Plus the fact that you've never called me in Kentucky to ask about things like spot cleaning. Plus, the tone of your voice when you said 'lipstick,' not to mention the implications of the word, and you said 'shirt,' not 'blouse.' Plus—"

"Mother," Peg said, "the last time I checked my wallet, *I* was the detective."

"Then I have nothing to be concerned about?"

"Nothing except this stain. Come on, Mother. There must be something I can do. Don't you have any down-home method for spots?"

"My down-home method," her mother said, "would be to try another dry cleaner."

CHAPTER THREE

"It doesn't look like much yet," Diane said as they got out of Peg's car in the cottage driveway. "Don't expect anything terrific."

"You keep telling me that." The wind off the Connecticut side of Long Island Sound was brutal, and Peg put her ungloved hands into her pockets. She followed Diane up the flagstone walk that was more frozen dirt than stones. The little house was old but pretty, with pinkish shingles and dark gray shutters. "The inside can't be as bad as you say."

"Oh, no? It took me a year to find a place I could afford, remember? On my pay you don't get hand-stained oak paneling."

"It needs a little paint, but I love it," Peg said. "It's darling. Plenty of windows, and there's room for a garden. And the beach right in your backyard —how wonderful. Could you open the door? I'm freezing."

"I'm trying. Ah—there." Diane got the brass knob to turn and they went in. "Home sweet squalor. What do you think?"

Peg looked around. The planked floor was uneven; paint hung from the ceiling in giant patches, and hammocks of cobweb were everywhere. She could see into the kitchen; the linoleum and fixtures seemed to have been installed during the Middle Ages. But the house had tons of potential.

"It's great," Peg said, looking up to admire a wrought-iron sconce and getting a string of web in her face.

"You don't mean it," Diane said.

"I do. I'm not just being polite. Certainly it's dirty and it needs a lot, but after you do everything you'll have a real house."

Diane smiled. "That's what I thought when I first saw it. What a load of work, though."

"But it's worthwhile for something like this. Your own *house*." She went to a back window and looked out. "The water right there, anytime you want it. I'm so jealous."

"Jealous?" Diane said. "Why, Peg? You don't even like the shore much."

"Not the shore—the whole thing." She shivered.

"Freezing in here, isn't it? That's why I haven't done much fixing up. You can only work so long in the cold. Your fingers get blue. Come on into the kitchen. I'll make some tea."

The square room held a decrepit wooden table and chairs. Peg sat down. She revised her estimate of how old the fixtures were as she got a look at the stove: it predated the Pleistocene Era.

"Wait a second," she said, hugging herself for warmth. "How come you don't have heat if the stove works?"

"Oil burner. There'll be a delivery sometime this week—then I'll move in. The stove is the only thing that uses gas. Hey, did you brush off that chair? It's filthy."

"No. But my coat can't get any dirtier." She looked down at the once-bright wool. "I think I've invented a new color. This is now 'grellow.' "

"Weren't you going to buy a new one?"

"I haven't had a chance."

The kettle whistled and Diane turned off the flame. She poured water over the bags in two mugs, put sugar on the table, and sat down.

"So," she said, "we got off the subject. What are you jealous of?"

"I told you," Peg said, dunking her tea bag. "The whole thing. You bought a *house*. That's so permanent, so—*committed*."

"My," Diane said, sipping gingerly. "You really *are* sick of Ron."

Peg laughed. "Good old Diane. You always know. Promise me we won't lose touch after you move."

"We won't. I don't want to either. What would I do for entertainment? Just watching you live your life is better than TV some days. Speaking of which," she said, brushing loose paint chips off the table, "who's the David Robertson on your calendar for Friday?"

Peg smiled. "Someone I have a date with. For dinner."

"He's taking you to dinner? That's an improvement over Ron right there. Where did you meet him?"

Peg looked into her cup. "At, uh, at work."

"He works at Smith-Clove?"

"No. He was shopping. This tea is delicious. What kind is it? I've never had it."

"You've had it two or three hundred times that I know of. It's pekoe, just like the tag says. This is getting interesting. Are you going to tell me how you met the guy, or do I have to drag it out of you one hilarious detail at a time?"

"Hilarious?" Peg said. "What makes you—"

"Peg." Diane tapped the back of her hand with a long rose fingernail. "Who do you think you're talking to, Mother Theresa? I know you always—"

There was a sudden bang outside the kitchen window. Both women jumped; Peg's mug fell. She ignored the tea dripping onto the floor as they raced to the back door.

The wind whipped their hair, stinging their faces. It had picked up while they were inside and was whining in the pine trees.

"Here," Diane said, pointing to a dangling chunk of windowsill. "The wind must have knocked it against the house. I'd better nail it down before it falls off all the way." She tried to fit it back into place, but it came off in her hand.

"Damn," Peg said. "Just what you need—another repair." She stuck her hands under her arms. "Why don't you get a hammer and nails, and I'll help you put it back up."

"No," Diane said, opening the back door. She motioned Peg in and followed her, carrying the piece of wood. "Whew! Take as cold as you've ever been, double it, and that's what life on the water is like. I can tell already."

"But the windowsill—"

"I'll do it when the sun comes out. Why risk frostbite when I can get away with just hypothermia?" She set the wood on the floor.

"What a mess," Peg said, looking at the tea on the linoleum. "Where are your paper towels?"

Diane took a roll from a cabinet and gave it to her. She left the room and came back with a bottle.

"Do you need this?" she asked. "It's stain remover. I don't have the money to replace that floor, so I've been trying to clean it."

"No, the tea is all off," Peg said. "A little water did the trick." Diane went back out. Peg threw away the used towels and sat down. Immediately she stood up again. "Stain remover?"

"What?" Diane said from the living room.

"Let me see that." She went to Diane and took the bottle. "Where's the rest of the label?"

Diane shrugged. "It must have worn off. You just rub the stuff into the stained area. Do it twice if you have to. It works, believe me. Do you need it? Take the bottle. Just give it back when you're done."

"Thanks," Peg said. She tucked it into her purse, covering her mouth to hide her smile. There wouldn't be another piece of banging windowsill to save her if Diane started asking questions again.

Oh, she'd talk about David eventually—but she'd feel silly if she raved on about him now and nothing much happened. Once they'd had a couple of dates, and he realized she was a perfectly normal person who didn't spend every day having tugs-of-war with shoplifters, getting lipstick on people's clothes, and falling deathly ill at lunch counters. . . .

"You're early," Peg said, smiling, at the open door. Behind her was her living room, all sunny prints and soft fabrics. The light from the lamps made the polished tables gleam.

David grinned back. "No inconvenience, I hope."

His voice—she had almost forgotten how lovely it was. It was an unexpected treat, like a surprise present.

"Definitely not," she said. "Come in."

She noticed he had a briefcase, but before she could puzzle that out she found herself with an armful of cashmere. She started to lay the coat over the couch, but stopped; David Robertson was a hanger man if ever she'd seen one.

She put the coat in the closet, pushing aside an ironing board, piled-up suitcases, and a stack of plant pots. The pots started to topple, and Peg grabbed the top few and put them on the floor, away from the coat. Where David was concerned, she was going to do things the neat way, the right way . . . the *only* way. Carelessness was for careless people like Ron. Now Ron was out of her life, and so was that quality.

She closed the closet door. "Well," she said. "Hello again."

David turned from the window. He wore a blue suit that wasn't quite navy, and the muted color highlighted his rich brown hair. All on their own Peg's X-ray eyes went inside the ivory shirt, beneath his pants, and found the glowing image of his bare skin. She saw his strong chest, his virile legs and buttocks. Just as it had at the lunch counter, his clothing seemed to melt away, exposing the David she'd admired so breathlessly through the two-way glass.

She clenched her teeth against a flush of shame. David didn't know her secret and never would. He was here in her apartment to take her out on a nice, ordinary date. She had to remember that, before the mental images rattled her into acting like an idiot.

She hardly knew the man. Seeing his naked body had been a complete accident. It was *not* available to her.

"I have it for you," David said.

Peg's eyes went wide. "You do?" she croaked.

"Mm-hm. Here." He opened his briefcase and took out the blue shirt. It was neatly folded inside a plastic bag.

Peg swallowed. She put her hand to her chest, as if that would make her heart rate drop back to normal. She'd forgotten about the shirt.

He handed it to her. "Did I tell you I'm really glad you're doing this? You wouldn't believe how much I love the shirt. I was mad as hell when the cleaners couldn't get the red out."

For the first time it occurred to Peg that she ought to be concerned about that. Unease simmered in her stomach.

Bug brain, she thought, where did you get the idea you could do better than some expensive dry cleaner? If he's that crazy about the shirt, he must have taken it to a top place. And if *they* gave up . . .

"This will be one dinner I'm real happy to pick up the tab for," David said. "Not that it isn't fun to take you out anyway"—he looked appreciatively over her bronze wool turtleneck dress, at the way the soft knit made the most of what curves she had —"but I arranged for a special way to say thanks." He smiled. "We have an eight o'clock reservation at Auberge Garfelle."

Auberge Garfelle! The plastic bag was growing moist where Peg clutched it. If she'd felt pressured before, now she was panicky. She'd never been to the Auberge, but Diane had, for her parents' anniversary. Breathtaking atmosphere, fine food, elegant service—and the cost for two would cover the down payment on a Porsche.

That bottle she'd borrowed had better contain a liquid miracle.

"How lovely," she said, forcing a smile. "I can't wait."

"Have you been there?"

"No," she said.

"Well, I go all the time, but on business. So this'll be a double treat for me—a chance to enjoy Auberge Garfelle with a pretty lady, and a way to thank you for your handy talent."

Trying not to choke, Peg went into the kitchen. The plastic bag was now so slippery she had to clutch it to herself to keep from dropping it.

She put it on the counter and slipped the shirt out. She took the stain remover from under the sink. Gently she unfolded the shirt and laid it on paper towels. She could see why David loved it: the blue was an unusual shade with a touch of smoky gray, and the fabric felt like a soft tissue. She hadn't known men's clothes could feel like that. Her father and two brothers back in Kentucky had plenty of shirts, but they were sturdy things you could make bean bags out of.

"Mind if I watch the expert at work?" David asked from right behind her, and she spun around with a gasp. "Oh, sorry," he said.

"That's okay. You just surprised me." She noticed his scent, an enticing blend of soap, aftershave, and just plain maleness. She had to ignore it; she had work to do. Whatever her chances were of getting out the lipstick, they shrank to worse than none with David for an audience.

"Actually," she said, "it, um, it's bad for my concentration if someone watches." *Not to mention my hormones.* "Just make yourself comfortable on the couch. Would you like some wine?"

"I'll wait till you're done, and you can have some with me."

Either that, Peg thought, or cyanide.

She put some stain remover on a paper towel and lifted the shirt cuff. It was clean; she took the other.

It was clean too.

Peg stood still for a minute, perplexed. Could he have brought the wrong shirt? No. David Robertson didn't seem like a man who ever even got a wrong number.

She held both cuffs and looked closely, turning them. Finally she saw it: a pale pink smudge, faint as could be. Oh, no. He considered *this* a stain?

Well, great. Terrific. She'd backed herself into some corners before, but this was the tightest yet. Here was her secret centerfold in her living room, whose interest she'd managed to spark even though their first meeting and seven eighths of their second had been disastrous, waiting to treat her to a dream evening at the most luxurious restaurant in Hartford, probably in all of Connecticut . . .

. . . and the only thing she had to do first was remove a spot so pale she'd cheerily have worn it smack on her collar, but which he considered an inkblot.

She sighed and began to rub.

"By the way," David asked from the living room, "how did you get into this?"

It was so much what she was wondering that it took Peg a minute to see what he meant.

"Oh," she said. "Spot cleaning."

"Did you ever work in a laundry or something?"

I wish. "No. Just a hobby."

There was a pause. "Your hobby is taking stains out of things?"

Peg clenched her teeth. She was straining so just to keep this invisible stain in view that she wasn't making sense.

"I mean, you know, a knack," she said. She made herself chuckle. "They say everyone's good at something."

"Isn't that the truth," he said, laughing. "You'll never guess what my special talent is."

"Microsurgery."

"What?"

"I said, I can't guess. What is it?"

"Rivers."

"Rivers?" She was only half listening. Nothing seemed to be happening to the spot, and she was frustrated and edgy. She put a little more stain remover on a fresh towel.

He laughed again. "I know the lengths of rivers. Don't ask me why."

I wasn't going to.

"Go ahead, name one."

"Name a river?" she asked. Her hand was getting tired. She started rubbing with her left.

"Sure. Any one. I'll tell you how long it is."

"The Mississippi."

"Two thousand three hundred and thirty miles. Name another."

"The, uh, Danube."

"One thousand seven hundred and thirty-six. Come on, give me a hard one."

Maybe Ron wasn't so bad after all. "Let's see— rivers. I don't know that many. How about—the Nile?"

"Huh," he said. "That's only the longest in the world. Four thousand one hundred sixty. Think of a really obscure one."

Peg squinted, trying to concentrate. She couldn't think of any obscure rivers. She couldn't think of any more rivers at all. If she had to keep up this rubbing much longer, she wouldn't be able to think of her *address*. Why had she ever said she'd do this? The stupid little thing would never come out, and she was a wreck. Between the fumes and her nerves and—

She couldn't see the stain.

She peered at the cuff, so close her nose almost touched it. There was no pink left.

"Well?" David asked.

"Just a second," she said.

She moved a chair under the fluorescent light and

stood on it. She held the cuff to the bulb and examined it from both sides. The stain was gone.

"Hallelujah," she said weakly. She climbed down and poured a touch more liquid on the paper towel, then ran it over the whole lower sleeve area to remove any bits of stain that might have spread as she was cleaning.

"Six hundred seventy-seven."

Peg looked out the kitchen door. "What?"

"The Vistula. It's six hundred—"

"What's the Vistula?"

David frowned. "The river you just named. It goes to the Gulf of—"

"I didn't say that. I said 'Hallelujah.' " Peg smiled. "I got the stain out."

"Good. Thanks," David said.

Peg's relief was so intense that his matter-of-fact tone hurt. But then she realized that of course he'd take her success in stride. *He* didn't know she was as adept at spot removal as she was at whale hunting. He'd come over to get his shirt cleaned, and she'd cleaned it.

"That dry cleaner must not have tried very hard," she couldn't resist saying, though her right hand felt paralyzed and her left just barely functional. An inspiration struck. "I'll dry this and it'll be good as new."

"Dry it? How?"

"With my hair dryer," she said, as though she did this twice a day. She went to get it.

Three minutes later she presented him with a pristine shirt. "Good as new," she said, trying not to look too triumphant.

"Great." He began to fold it. "Where's the bag?"

"Oh, don't put it away," Peg said impulsively. "Wear it."

"You mean now?"

"Sure. It's all nice and clean, and it'll look wonderful with that suit."

"Well," he said, looking down at his beige shirt, "this *was* a substitute. And the tie will go with it. Okay." He headed for the bedroom. "I'll change in here."

Too bad apartments don't have two-way mirrors, Peg thought as she cleaned up the kitchen. She put the stain remover back under the sink. Tomorrow she'd go to Old Lyme and return it to Diane, who had moved the last of her belongings into the beach house and was madly scrubbing. And she'd tell her about David, now that things seemed to be chugging along.

She felt so much lighter! Even the river business seemed charming, now that the strain was over. Well, this was the way to go, no doubt about it. She was going to be really careful not to get into any more tense, embarrassing situations with this exciting man.

David came out. The blue shirt enhanced the effect of the suit on his skin and eyes; if he had been attractive before, now he was magnificent. He put the ivory shirt into his briefcase. Watching him snap it shut, Peg realized why he'd brought it: what else would he carry the shirt in? Nobody as well dressed and conventional as David would walk around with a paper bag or a canvas tote—or just hold the thing in his hand, as she would have done.

She poured Chablis and they relaxed on the couch for a few minutes. At seven thirty-five David said it was time to go.

Peg got their coats from the closet. He helped her into hers, holding it in just the right position, and they went out. He led her to a Lincoln Continental parked in front of her building. She couldn't see the color well in the dark, but the car gleamed as though it had just been waxed. He tucked her trailing coat corner inside before closing the door. It shut with a luxurious *thwump*.

Peg didn't know whether David had reserved the table specially or if it was a lucky accident, but they were seated at a window wall overlooking the city. From the thirtieth-floor restaurant, the lights of the parkway cloverleafs were like a tangle of bright bracelets, and cars wove steady patterns of red and white. They could see the Ramada Inn, the Hilton, and the golden dome of the capitol building.

"How beautiful," Peg said. "I feel like we're in a plane."

David laughed. "The food's a lot better. Are you hungry?"

"Starved." She took a sculpted mushroom from a dish of iced vegetables that had been served with the wine David ordered. She smiled at him. He smiled back and touched her hand.

"Your skin is so smooth," he said quietly. His rich voice was even sexier when he lowered it that way, and she trembled briefly, trying not to think of *his* skin. The trailing touch became a caress as his fingers went inside her sleeve and circled her wrist.

The waiter came and explained the evening's specials. David kept his hand where it was, warming hers.

"I've had the poached salmon appetizer," he said when the waiter left. "It's delicious. And the cream of sorrel soup is excellent, but they serve a big bowl. It might be too filling for you. What are you having for an entree?"

"I was thinking of the steak au poivre," Peg said. It was a wonder she could think of anything coherent with him stroking her hand like that. Even the light touch had her senses spinning. She was being pulled deeper and deeper into David's sensuous aura.

"They do it very well," he said, "but it's a lot of food."

"That's all right," Peg said. He'd taken his hand away. She missed it, but at least she could talk again. "I have a big appetite. I eat a lot."

"As long as it's not liver," he said, grinning.

Peg looked away. "Let's go back to the steak au poivre."

David made her face him with a firm hand on her jaw. "Don't be upset. I was flattered."

"You were?" she asked. "I thought you were just uncomfortable."

"Well," he said, caressing her cheek, "I can't deny that. I meet you twice, and twice I find myself involved in a spectacle. The first time I kind of asked for it—but the second time I was just sitting there minding my business when all of a sudden a woman finds me so interesting it causes her to order a sandwich she hates."

Peg turned away again, and again he made her face him. "Can't you see why I was flattered? It's not every day I have that effect on a woman."

Peg thought, If you only knew what a spectacle you were involved in the first time we *really* met. And speaking of your effect on a woman. . . .

He went on. "And I did get to meet you again."

"Well," Peg said, "considering how the first time went, at Smith-Clove, I guess *I* should be flattered that you didn't get up and change your seat when I —er, when we ran into each other at the deli."

David sat back in the cushioned blue armchair. "You know," he said, "I've been thinking about that shoplifting business. I probably shouldn't have interfered."

"Oh," Peg said, surprised. "Thanks. You're nice to say so."

He shrugged. "I stopped to help someone who seemed to need it, the way you stop on the road when you see a car broken down. Then it escalated, and I got mad. That guy you work with—what's his name?"

"Hugh Burgholtz."

"Burgholtz. Right. He's some scurvy little guy. He ticked me off. But I realized later I should have paid more attention to what you said. I was too rude. I should have respected your methodology."

"My—methodology?"

"Sure. You tried to tell me the situation wasn't what it looked like. How do I know a shoplifter from a grand piano? This is your profession. You have your procedures, your established structure. It wasn't up to me to mess with it, any more than you or Burgholtz could be expected to negotiate a corporate lease."

She wasn't going to tell him that terms like "methodology," "procedures," and "structure" were no more a part of how she did her job than Hungarian proverbs were. What he'd said was basically right, and it was decent of him to apologize. One more thing to like.

The waiter came back, and they ordered. David said, "So you decided on the soup and steak. Where do you put it all? You're so slim."

Peg shrugged. "Just lucky. I never put on weight. My roommate hates me."

"You have a roommate?"

"Actually she's not my roommate anymore. She just bought a house."

David said, "That's interesting."

"It really is," Peg said. "She got a beach cottage in Old Lyme. It's prehistoric, and Diane is up to her hips in dust and flaking paint, but it's a house and it's *hers.*"

"I didn't mean the house." He leaned over to stroke her neck, and she felt his thigh against hers briefly, warmly. "I meant it's interesting that you're living by yourself now."

He looked her full in the eyes, a look heavy with possibility, with intent, with promise. For a wild moment Peg wished the whole room and everyone in it would melt away and leave only herself and David, and David's wonderful body and his mouth. He'd lean over all the way and it would meet hers in a lovely exploring kiss. The hand on her neck would move into her hair to hold her while his kiss went deeper, sparking sweet warmth from her toes all the way up . . . the way his eyes and fingers were doing now, only much more so.

Fortunately their appetizers came, and Peg busied herself with her soup, glad for the familiar motions of eating while she struggled for composure.

She'd begun to fear for her advertised appetite while David was touching her, but when her steak came she found herself ravenous. For dessert she had apricot soufflé. David had white chocolate mousse and Irish coffee. He held out his coffee glass for a taste, but Peg shook her head.

"Take some. Go ahead, before the whipped cream melts," he urged.

"No, thanks," she said. "I don't like Irish whiskey."

"Is that why you didn't order one? You should have told me." He called the waiter over. "What kind of liqueur do you like?" David asked her. "We'll get you a coffee made with that instead."

"Let's see," she said. "What's the licorice one? Anisette."

"Anisette coffee," the waiter said, and left.

David took a sip from his glass. As he set it down, Peg saw something drop. She frowned and looked closer. It was a small white button.

David didn't notice. He said, "Tell me how you came to be a detective. Is it something you always wanted to do?"

"I wanted a career that was analytical. I like to piece things together. And I'm quite—inventive," she said, using as polite a term as she could for the impulsive, adventurous quality that some people, such as her boss, had more insulting ways of describing. "In college I majored in philosophy because I liked it . . ." Her voice ran down as she saw there was something odd about David's wrist when he raised his glass again. Oh, his cuff was open, that was it. Because of the fallen button.

"Yes?" he prompted. "And what did you do after you graduated?"

"I tutored undergraduates." What *was* the problem with his shirt? She took a breath to mention it, but he was talking again.

"You tutored them in philosophy?"

"Philosophy and math. Listen, I think your—"

"Math? I'm impressed. You must have some fine analytical mind. That should make you a great detective."

She didn't answer.

"And inventiveness is another asset in your kind of work."

Peg couldn't speak. She felt she might choke. She was mortified. All the inventiveness in the world wasn't going to get her out of the sickening fix she'd just landed in. And David still hadn't noticed what was happening to his shirt. It was as if they were both watching a monster movie whose plot only she knew. Her stomach was rolling with her knowledge of what he was about to see.

"I guess you have some fascinating experiences to tell about," he said, raising a hand to scratch his cheek. "How do you—good God."

He stared at his wrist, then at Peg with horror, then down again. He was looking at his sleeve, at the button that had come off and was lying on the tablecloth.

The reason it had come off was that the fabric it was sewn to was no longer there. Long shreds of cotton dangled over his wrist and hand like a scarecrow's fringe. Sprinkles of blue littered the table. As they watched, still more of the sleeve disintegrated into little piles.

"What," he asked, his breath making the fabric bits swirl between them, "did you use on this?"

Peg swallowed. Her hands, held tightly together in her lap, were wet. She prayed to faint.

"Sp-spot remover," she said, barely able to get the words out. "My roommate—"

"Check, please," David said curtly to the goggle-eyed waiter, who had just brought Peg's coffee. He turned back to her. "I thought you knew what you were doing. You said you had a knack for getting stains out. You *offered* to clean my shirt."

"I know," she said miserably. "I—"

"How could you do this?" he demanded, his voice low but clipped with fury. "I came to your apartment carrying a stained shirt in my briefcase. Now I'm in a public place, a dignified restaurant where the staff knows me. I'm not carrying the shirt, I'm wearing it, and it's not stained, it's *tattered!*" His gray eyes beamed his rage. "*How dare you embarrass me like this?*"

"David, please believe me, I never meant—"

"Forget it," he said disgustedly. The long trails of blue swung madly as he scribbled his name on the credit card slip. I should have known, he thought furiously. I should never have trusted this flake to do anything but destroy the shirt.

Peg sniffed back tears. "Just let me—"

"Don't talk to me, all right? Don't say another word. Come on."

They were getting out of here. His beautiful shirt was a disaster. So was this night. So was this *woman*. He should have known.

Peg followed David as he strode out of the restaurant, past what seemed to be its entire staff, all trying valiantly not to notice the shreds hanging from the wrist he held awkwardly against his side.

CHAPTER FOUR

"Acetic acid," Peg said into the phone.

"I've never heard of it," Diane said.

"I hadn't either, but David knew all about it. He could read enough of that torn label to tell the bottle isn't stain remover—it's stuff they use in photography. They put pictures in it after developing them, to fix the image."

"Oh-ho," Diane said. "My mother gave it to me, but she must have gotten it from my brother; he does photography. So it contains acid? How come it doesn't eat a picture if it can eat a shirt?"

"I don't know," Peg said. She rubbed her eyes. She felt terrible. "I don't understand any of it, except that I tried to help the man and instead I—I—"

"Demolished him."

"It was so awful when he brought me home. I kept trying to apologize, but he wouldn't listen. I've never seen anyone so mad. His face looked like a volcano. He grabbed the bottle, read it, yelled at me, and slammed out. I could hear his car screech away from in here."

"And he didn't call today."

"No. He's never going to call again."

"You're probably right," Diane said helpfully.

"Oh, stop!"

"I'm just being realistic," her ex-roommate said. "You always tell me I keep your feet on the ground."

"Sometimes," Peg grumbled, "it's an act of mercy to leave them in the air. Anyway, I'm not the only one being flaky this time. Who gave me a photographic product and said it was stain remover?"

"It *is*. You should see my bathroom light fixture. All the rust and spots came off. You didn't say you were going to use the stuff on fabric. I'd as soon have given you a blowtorch."

Peg sat down at the kitchen table. She'd been trying to put away dishes as she talked, but she was messing it up, sticking things in the wrong cabinets.

"His shirt looks like I used one," she said. "And then a machine gun for good measure."

"I'm really sorry. I just think of that bottle as something my mother uses for heavy cleaning. You know, a lot of products that aren't meant to clean do a great job. Peanut butter, for one."

"You can *clean* with that?"

"Sure," Diane said. "It does chrome like magic. You take a cloth—"

"Never mind," Peg said. "I'd just ruin somebody's Mercedes with it. Hey, do I hear barking?"

"I forgot to tell you. That's Blondie. I adopted her yesterday."

"Congratulations! You finally got a dog. What kind?"

"She's a mutt. Light and fuzzy and kind of foxy-looking. She's only ten weeks old."

"She sounds adorable," Peg said.

"She is. Want to meet her? I'll bring her over one of these evenings."

"Anytime," Peg said. "I'll just be here hating myself."

His new blue shirt had french cuffs and the color was a hair different—but it was the best he was going to do, David Robertson told himself as he finished knotting his tie and gathered the shirt wrapping paper to throw away. He'd searched for a duplicate, but after two weeks he'd given up. His clients wouldn't enjoy letting their properties stand empty while he pursued a second career in shirt hunting.

He straightened his already straight bedroom, checked the thermometer outside the window, and took his coat, muffler, and gloves from the hall closet. He used the house phone to ask Hassan, the building garage attendant, to bring the car around.

It had snowed a dusting during the night, but by now the gale that seemed to be daily February fare had dispersed the powder, and the roads were dry. The Lincoln was warm, thanks to Hassan's knowledge of his routine, and he drove along in comfort, his thoughts drifting.

Where they drifted immediately, as they did whenever he got into the car now, was to Peg Bailey. He didn't recall her perfume being especially strong that Friday night, but it seemed to be in the car's pores. Every time the heat went on, he smelled it.

At first he'd been livid. He'd wanted to fumigate

the damn car, anything to get rid of this reminder of her. After a week it had just been *there*, part of the Lincoln, like the gearshift. But now . . . now something weird was happening. He *enjoyed* the smell. When he got in, it settled around him like a silky cloud.

He'd never been as mad as he was that night, with his best shirt hanging in shreds while he stalked out of the most elegant place in the city trying to keep some dignity. He'd felt humiliated, used, made a fool of. He had no idea why a woman would claim she was good at stain removal and then make his shirt look as though it had been swallowed and digested. All he knew was that he never wanted to see the incompetent space cadet again.

But somehow, inexplicably, his anger had faded. He was actually starting to miss Peg. He'd been with her three times, and each time she'd practically managed to incite a world war; he who loathed calling attention to himself inevitably landed in the spotlight in some insane way. That routine would certainly have to go if . . . what?

If he began seeing her.

Once the thought was out in the open, he was so startled he hit the brake, then winced as a horn blew chidingly behind him. Good lord, even *thinking* of the woman put him in an embarrassing position.

But he knew immediately that it was what he wanted. Her pretty, cheery face . . . the satiny skin of her hands that made him wonder what the rest of her was like . . . her bubbly personality, her comments, her jokes . . . and the slender but so feminine shape, the graceful way she moved, like a deer. . . . He missed all that, wanted it again as it had been—a beginning, a heady promise.

He breathed deeply once, then again. He'd never known a smell could be so magical.

On the way into his office building, he realized he was grinning. He made his face blank and glanced around, but no one was staring. He walked faster, eager to get upstairs. He was definitely going to do it. He was going to call Peg.

It was hard not to start smiling again as he thought about how surprised she'd be to hear from him.

"Good morning, Mr. Robertson."

"Good morning, Miss Lewis. Cold out." He continued past his secretary into his office and took off his coat.

There was a pink message slip on his desk. He'd return that call and then phone Smith-Clove. He thought about hearing Peg's voice again. She sure was going to be one amazed store detective.

He sat down, glanced at the slip, reached for the phone, and then looked again. It had Peg's name and the store number.

Well, how about that? He smiled to himself, a big one now that he was alone. He'd been hoping she wouldn't shriek too deafeningly with surprise when she heard from him, while all along. . . .

He had to admire her. How many people in her situation would have the courage to do anything but crawl into a cave and stay there? Yet here she was, dusting herself off and calling him. She *was* an upbeat, optimistic, go-for-it person—that was a lot of what was so nice about her. And also . . .

Oh, admit it. He liked that she wasn't shy about showing her interest. He wished he could be more like that himself. Women saw him as distant and a little stuffy, he knew; he dealt expertly with people in real estate, but take off his tie and put a drink in his hand, and he tended to behave as if he were still in a corporate conference.

He called Smith-Clove and got through to Peg right away.

"David!" she said. "I'm glad you called me back. I was afraid you wouldn't."

"You were?" he asked foolishly, her voice making him feel hot and cold at once.

"Definitely. But I was hoping you'd have calmed down enough to let me apologize—which I'd like to do by buying you another shirt."

"I appreciate that," he said, touched. "But I already bought one."

"Oh," she said.

She sounded so disappointed that he immediately wanted to make her feel better. "It's a great shirt. I like it better than the old one," he lied.

"You *do?* What a relief. I've been so upset. Listen, I'm going to pay you for it."

"No way," he said. He didn't point out that on the money she probably made, it would be like buying a major kitchen appliance. "Forget the shirt. I'd just like to pick up where we left off. Are you free tonight?"

"Yes," she said promptly, delighting him.

"How does a movie and pizza sound?"

"Oh," she said, "it sounds *wonderful.*"

He laughed. "Relax. It's not a European cruise." But maybe someday. "I'll come for you at six."

"Make it six thirty. I've been working like mad on a theft case, and I won't be leaving till six."

He hung up, as pleased as if he'd just drawn his commission on a five-year lease.

"Green and red peppers?" David asked her.

"Mmm. And mushrooms?"

"Right." He gave the waiter the order, adding extra cheese and a bottle of Chianti.

What she really loved on pizza was garlic slivers, but not tonight. She'd sworn to do nothing even remotely embarrassing with David; risking garlic breath was out.

Even a thick-skinned person would have been uncomfortable with all the crazy things she'd made happen; for someone as particular as David, she'd been a walking land mine. Well, that was over. She was on her most perfect behavior. She wouldn't even get a speck of pizza sauce on her new gold sweater.

"That's the funniest movie I've seen in months, even if it is an old one," David said. "The operating room scene had me on the floor."

"It was terrific. Only Woody Allen could make surgery so funny."

"I'm glad you like him. A lot of people don't." He smiled. "Something we share. Besides pizza toppings. Mmm, here it is."

The waiter set the pan down. The cheese was still bubbling, and the oregano smell made Peg's mouth water. David pulled some slices apart to cool, and

67

cheese oozed onto the pan. Peg couldn't wait; she took some on her finger. It was burning hot.

Suddenly her finger was in David's mouth.

The moist heat of his tongue was so lovely, she immediately forgot the pain that had stung for a second before his mouth soothed it away.

"Dodo," he said affectionately, still holding her hand, "you weren't kidding about your appetite. You risked a first-degree burn to get at that cheese."

"Really?" she said. The word sounded like gibberish in her ear. She was surprised she could get it out at all. She couldn't focus on anything but the thrum of her pulse, the thrill of his protective yet intimate gesture. Her finger tickled where his tongue had been. She wished it were still there.

As if he'd read the thought, David pulled her hand to his lips again and kissed the backs of her fingers. Peg closed her eyes.

Then she opened them wide. Her bra had just come unhooked.

His tug on her hand had done it, made the front clasp that was sometimes a problem snap open. Now her arm froze in midair. The bra was still more or less on, but if she moved her arms much, it would shift, and her misfortune would be on display. People often complimented her slim but curvaceous figure—but only she knew her curves were very dependent on a good supportive bra.

She made herself smile winningly at David while she slowly brought her arm back so that she was holding both elbows close in to her chest, her shoulders hunched over a little. At least she'd look normal while she searched for a way to handle this.

David picked up a pizza slice and neatly flipped strings of cheese back onto it. "It's cool enough to eat," he said, holding it out.

"Uh, no, thanks," she said.

"Take it," he urged, holding it closer.

Peg opened her mouth to answer, then shut it when no answer presented itself. She couldn't think what to do. She didn't want to embarrass herself by moving her arms and dislodging her bra completely —and she didn't want to embarrass David by ducking under the table or going into some bizarre contortion to close it surreptitiously.

"I don't—I'm not quite ready yet," she said.

David frowned. "You were ready enough to forfeit a couple of layers of skin a minute ago."

She forced a chuckle. "Appetites are such changeable things, aren't they? First you're starved, then you don't feel like eating."

"You're really not hungry anymore?"

The spicy, cheesy smell drifted around her in a delicious cloud. The browned mozzarella on David's slice glistened with olive oil. The oregano-flecked crust looked light and crunchy. Her mouth filled with saliva.

"No," she said, shaking her head. "Not at all."

David ate his pizza, watching her with concern. Peg was pretty concerned herself. Mainly she was concerned about how in the wide green world she was ever going to get out of this.

"I think," she said as casually as she could, "I'll go to the ladies' room for a second."

Instantly David was half out of his seat. "You feel sick?"

"Oh, no. I'm just going to take a little walk over there, that's all."

"Peg, you're not making sense," he said. "You say you're not sick, but suddenly you don't want to eat."

Standing up, Peg started to shrug, to show him how big a deal this wasn't. Feeling the bra start to shift past the point of no return, she yanked her elbows back to her chest and resumed her slump.

David said, "You're doubling over. What *is* it? Please let me help?" He slid out of the booth and came around to her side. He gripped her shoulders.

Peg leaned over farther, holding her arms in tight.

"Where's the pain?" he whispered.

Their waiter came over. "Is the lady sick?" he asked. "Does she need a doctor?"

"Peg," David coaxed, "tell me where it hurts."

"It—doesn't," she choked out.

"What do you mean, it doesn't? You're obviously in terrible pain."

"Should I call an ambulance?" the waiter asked worriedly.

Peg closed her eyes. Now she *was* starting to feel sick—sick and tired of the way David Robertson's presence seemed to cause her to wreak havoc every time.

Her hands were sweaty. Her back ached from her hunched-over position. She was worrying the heck out of David, and he clearly wasn't going to get out of her way so she could get to the ladies' room. She had to tell him.

"My bra is open," she whispered.

"What?" David said. He leaned in closer. The waiter leaned in too.

She turned her face to David and said even more softly, "My bra is open."

He said, "But what's *wrong?*"

The waiter stared anxiously, waiting for information.

"That's what's wrong," she said.

He let go of her shoulders.

"What is it?" the waiter asked.

David looked helplessly at Peg.

The poor waiter seemed stricken. She had to reassure him before he called an undertaker.

"Could you bring me a glass of water?" she asked. "I'd feel much better if I had water."

He hurried away. She turned back to David. Now he had that look on his face, the one she'd seen when she got lipstick on his shirt, when she'd tasted the liver sandwich, when his cuff had disintegrated before his eyes. The look that said he'd give his Lincoln to be somewhere else.

"I don't understand," he whispered tightly.

Again she stopped herself from shrugging. She could hardly give him an anatomy lesson right now; obviously he was used to more naturally beautiful women.

"All I can tell you," she whispered back, "is that I need to get to the ladies' room to fix it." She wasn't sure how she could do that, all huddled over like a turtle, but while she was trying to straighten just enough to walk there without attracting more than two thirds of the other diners' attention, David

71

solved the problem. He took off his jacket and discreetly looked away while he helped her into it.

She was back in the booth in a minute, upset but intact. "I'm really sorry," she said, taking a pizza slice. She bit into it.

"Don't sweat it," David said. "Good, you're eating. You had me worried there."

The waiter came over. He looked at Peg, then at the untouched glass of water at her plate. She picked it up and took a big drink.

"Are you all right now?" the man asked.

"Oh, yes," she said. "Thank you."

"There was nothing wrong with the pizza?"

"The pizza? No. It's wonderful."

He waited. He seemed to expect her to go on.

"*Really* wonderful," she said, smiling brightly.

Still he waited.

"I, uh, wasn't myself for a minute," she said as truthfully as she could.

He nodded uncertainly and went away. Peg looked at David and shrugged, fully this time.

"I don't know why these things always happen when I'm with you," she said. "I feel terrible."

"Don't. You had me going, but I think I'm learning to handle it. Could you just—clarify for me what happened?" he asked, his gray eyes earnest.

She finished her third slice. "Well," she said, "if you can imagine a balloon . . ." No. That wouldn't explain anything.

He waited expectantly.

"Support," she said. "It's a question of support. Like a bridge, or a—" She'd been about to say "sling," but the comparison was too gross. She wanted to answer his question, not send him away screaming.

"Some women," she began again, "are naturally . . . firm. They can go without a bra and look like they're wearing one."

He seemed to be getting the idea.

"And some," she finished bravely, "can't." She lifted the last piece of pizza.

"I see," he said.

Flushing, she busied herself gathering up scraps from the pan. Another socko performance: here she was with the man she'd sworn not to disgrace, eating greasy mushrooms with her fingers while discussing the demerits of her breasts.

David tipped her chin up. "Don't let this bother you," he said. "It's over." She looked down again, and again he forced her to face him. "I know that was hard. Maybe I shouldn't have made you explain. But I'm glad you trust me enough to be so honest."

He paid the check and they went out to the car. When David asked if she'd like to see his apartment, she hesitated only a microsecond before saying yes. Any man honorable enough to listen with studious attention while she detailed her figure faults and not make one joke wouldn't think she was asking to be jumped if she came over.

Besides, she wished David *would* behave a touch less honorably. She didn't want things to progress too fast, but it was harder than ever to keep those thoughts away—the memory of David without his clothes, moving around the small room in an unknowing performance, just for her. . . .

73

They pulled into the circular drive of a white brick high rise. Lush evergreen plantings flanked oversize black glass doors with ivory handles. A gray-uniformed young man came out. He was short and trim, with skin the color of coffee with cream, and lots of black hair combed into a high wave.

"That's Hassan," David said, "our doorman and garage attendant. He's a bit of a character."

"Oh? In what way?"

David sighed. Peg had an impression of long-suffering patience. "You'll see."

Hassan opened Peg's door. "Evening, lady," he said, giving his hand to help her out.

"Hassan, this is Miss Bailey," David said.

"Hi," Peg said.

"Lady Bailey," he acknowledged, his smile widening. He turned to David. "Not happening moch you breeng lady home. Thees good lady. I can tell."

David's face tightened. "Hassan, if you don't mind."

"Nice short," the man said, tilting his head to see inside David's open coat. "Is being good color. Ladies like blue. I know." He flashed his grin again as he got into the driver's seat and shot the car into the garage with a screech.

David rolled his eyes and led Peg into the lobby. It was even lovelier than the entrance, with rosy mirrored walls and thick plum carpeting. Three velvet couches on carved ivory feet made an attractive sitting area.

The elevator door opened immediately and they went in. David shrugged off his coat.

"I think Hassan's nice," Peg said. "And he's right —that is a nice shirt."

They got out at the twentieth floor. "Like it?" David asked as he unlocked his door. "It's the replacement."

Peg looked again. "The blue isn't the same."

"It's close enough. Come on in."

The entry area was a wide foyer with a hutch of oak and glass and an oriental rug. They walked through it into the living room, and Peg's eyes widened. David had a corner unit, and two full walls were windowed, with a balcony running all around. The room was decorated in smoky browns with touches of bright red. A high-tech red-and-yellow kitchen could be seen beyond a dining bar with padded seats that were suspended from the ceiling on thick braided rope.

"This is incredible," Peg said. She turned to David. "I sound so naive. I guess I should act cool, but I can't help showing it—I'm impressed."

He laughed. "Good. I wanted to impress you. That's why I asked you here. How about coffee?"

"I'd love some."

David went into the kitchen, and Peg sat on one of the hanging seats and watched him. He took down cups and a jar of instant coffee and spooned it out. She was surprised; she'd expected custom-ground Ethiopian beans and some mysterious gourmet brewing device. Well, good. So he was elegant without being pretentious.

The kettle whistled, and David poured. He brought the cups over, put out milk and sugar, and sat next to Peg.

She sipped her coffee. It was way too strong. She poured in milk, then more milk. It didn't seem to affect it much.

"I apologize again for that—problem tonight," she said. "I promised myself nothing would happen."

David drank some coffee. He seemed to find nothing wrong with it. "I survived," he said, but his casual tone masked a jolt of discomfort at the reminder. He was trying to be understanding, but, damn it, he *did* wish she wouldn't do so many wacko things.

Well, maybe that would ease off as they got to know each other better. She seemed as upset as he was by the scenes she got into, so maybe she was trying to change that quality.

He stroked her brown curls. Peg winced inwardly. She'd loaded on more gel after work; her hair looked okay, but it felt like barbed wire.

David's brow wrinkled for a second, but he seemed to decide not to let a little thing like petrified hair bother him. He moved his hand down to her neck and caressed it.

His eyes held hers, and Peg didn't look away. She didn't want to break the current between them. She remembered the night at Auberge Garfelle, when David had held her chin and looked at her this way, and she'd felt a message that had made her tremble. *I'd be kissing you right now,* he'd said wordlessly, *if we weren't in a crowded public restaurant. I'd be taking you in my arms for the first time and meeting your lips with mine, your tongue with mine. . . .*

But they weren't in public now, and he leaned

over and gripped her shoulders as, finally, the kiss she'd dreamed and fantasized became stunning reality.

She'd imagined this so often, it was as if it had already happened. His mouth, familiar by now in its gentle intimacy, covering hers . . . his hands stroking her back, perhaps his fingers brushing her face. He might pause and hold her cheek to his, and she'd stretch up and put her arms around his neck, wanting him to kiss her again. . . .

But it wasn't like that at all. The quiet sweetness she'd expected was a trembling hunger instead. His mouth was all over her face, kissing her eyes, nipping her ear, tasting the corners of her lips with his warm tongue.

I'm not the only one who's been dreaming, Peg thought joyously as David pulled her close. The way he held her and touched her made it clear he'd waited for this too. The tension she felt in his whole body was the thrilling giveaway. It told her what he hadn't, that he was burning to know her in lovers' language, move ahead, move beyond. And she knew, too, that he cared too much to let those feelings run riot. She sensed his determination to be patient. He wouldn't rush her, no matter how badly he wanted to.

Long, lovely minutes later, as if confirming what she felt, David pulled back and held Peg gently away from him. He seemed to be marshaling his willpower.

But then, one last time, he bent and kissed her long and deeply, his tongue aggressive and exciting. Peg was spinning inside, her emotions a-tumble,

77

when he released her again and moved determinedly back, holding only her hands.

"That's been a long time coming," he said, his breathing rough. "I knew that once I got my hands on you it would be hell to stop—and it is." He pulled on her wrists to bring her near and kissed her softly on the lips.

"That'll have to hold me till I get back," he said.

"Back?" Peg asked. She picked up her coffee, took a swallow, resisted the impulse to make a face, and put it down.

"Didn't I tell you?" David said, draining his cup. "I'm going to the Virgin Islands to look at some properties."

"The Virgin Islands? How wonderful," she said with an enthusiasm she didn't feel. All she wanted was to keep kissing him every day, and he was leaving the country. "Is that what you bought the bathing suit for?"

"Partly." He looked at her cup. "Don't you want any more?"

"No, thanks," she said. "It keeps me up."

"You should have told me. I have decaf. Want some now?"

"Uh, no, I've had enough."

He took their cups to the sink. "I bought the suit for this trip, but I needed a new one anyway. There's an indoor pool on the roof here. Sometimes in the evening I—" He shut off the water and turned to look at her. "How did you know I bought a bathing suit?"

The sudden quiet was like a boom of thunder. Peg's heart seemed to freeze in her chest. She started to put her hand over her mouth but dropped it and gripped her other hand instead, squeezing.

"I—you told me," she said.

"No, I didn't. I didn't tell anybody."

"Yes. You—oh, I remember," she stammered. "At the store. Your bag—"

He came into the living room. "I never opened my bag."

Peg prayed for an explanation. She wished desperately that she'd prepared for this possibility.

"You must have." She forced a choked laugh. "Otherwise how would I know?"

"I remember everything that happened," David said, "and I definitely didn't open the bag."

"Well," she said. She tried for another chuckle, but didn't come close. "I'm sure we'll figure it out sooner or later. Could I change my mind about that decaf? I decided I—"

"In a minute. Peg, is it my imagination, or are you hiding something? I'd like to get to the bottom of this, but you seem reluctant."

Now she almost did laugh—the laugh of the doomed. She was "reluctant" to get to the bottom of this, all right—as reluctant as she'd be to swim the Everglades naked.

She squeezed her hands tighter, trying to think, getting nowhere.

David said, "Talk to me. What's the story?"

"I— Couldn't we just forget this?"

"Forget *what?*" he asked, exasperated. "I simply want to find out how you knew I bought a bathing suit."

She turned away. Her breath was catching in her throat. "I can't tell you."

His mouth became an angry line. "Don't play games. Tell me what's going on!"

"David, please—"

"Tell me, now! How the *hell* do you know about my suit?"

She opened her mouth but no words came out, and it stayed open.

"Answer me, damn it!" He came closer. He didn't touch her, but his voice was like a pistol shot.

She let out her breath. "I—saw you," she said.

"Saw me when? Where?"

"In the dressing room."

"What?" he said. "How could—oh, for God's sake. What the hell do you people do, watch us on TV or something?"

"No," Peg said indignantly. "We're supposed to keep the dressing rooms under surveillance. It's part of the job."

"What type of surveillance?"

"Just—checking."

"Well," he demanded, pacing the carpet, "where do you get off walking past men's dressing rooms?"

"I wasn't walking past." She swallowed. "And— they weren't men's."

He stared at her, his hands on his hips. He was silent while he tried to piece it together.

"If you weren't walking past," he asked finally with quiet rage, "where were you?"

She looked away. "On the other side of the mirror. It's one-way glass. It—"

"Wait a minute!" he yelled.

Peg's head snapped back.

"Did you say they weren't men's?"

"Yes," she said. "You were in a women's dressing room."

His face went rigid. "That's impossible."

"No. It's true."

"It can't be true!" He began to pace again. "Men can't walk into a women's dressing room!"

"You're right, they can't—but you did."

"No way. I—"

"*Yes*, David. The sign was smack in front of you. You stared right at it. It says, These ladies' fitting rooms monitored by female security personnel."

He turned away. Peg watched his back muscles stiffen and flex with his agonized tension as he replayed the scene in his mind. She could almost see him remembering each move, how every stitch had come off as he tried on the two suits—only this time he was picturing himself undressing and trying them on with feminine eyes tracking him.

He had to know it all, how humiliating it really was. "You were right up close to that mirror?" he asked without turning. "You saw—everything?"

Peg nodded.

"*Well?*"

"*Yes.*"

Now he faced her. "How could you?" he asked incredulously. "How could you stand there and do nothing while a man walked into a women's changing area—and then *watch him?* Is that your idea of fun?"

"No, of course not," Peg said softly through her choked throat. "Please understand, David—I didn't

81

want to make it worse for you by barging in and shocking you. I thought you'd just leave the store and never know."

He was looking at her as though he couldn't imagine why he'd ever thought she was sane.

"What could I have done?" she pleaded. "What would you have done?"

"Anything," he said, chopping the air with his hand. "*Anything*—but what you did. You could have made an announcement, sent a male detective in; you could have put up unmistakable signs in the first place, so this wouldn't happen. But the main thing I would have done," he yelled, pointing his finger at her, "was turn around! *Not watch!*"

Peg had no answer for that. She felt the sting of tears and blinked.

She'd made a miserable mess of everything. This time it looked as if she'd repelled David for good. He'd been irritated before, he'd been angry before— but now he was enraged.

"I guess I'll go," she said.

He strode to the coat closet. "I'll take you home."

"No," she said. She went to the closet herself and got her yellow coat and put it on. "I'll get a cab downstairs."

"I'll take you," he said, louder.

"*No.*" She couldn't bear another ride like the one after they'd been to Auberge Garfelle, when he'd driven her home alternately yelling and seething.

She tried the doorknob. It wouldn't move. She looked at the assorted hardware on the door and turned a couple of things, but it still didn't budge.

David came over, flipped one lever, and opened it, not looking at her.

"I'm sorry," Peg said, and left before he could answer.

"Lady Bailey," Hassan said, smiling as he held the door for her. He looked past her for David. "Mr. Robertson is forget to calling me for car. I get it." He started toward the garage.

"Wait," Peg said. "He didn't forget to calling. Uh, to call. He's not"—she took a slow breath to fight off tears—"he's not coming down. Can you get me a taxi?"

Hassan gaped. "He homing you in *taxi?*" he asked, clearly ready to run upstairs and teach the man a thing or two.

"*I* want to go home in a taxi," Peg said firmly.

Hassan squinted at her and decided she meant business. "Floor sure," he said. He pushed some buttons on the lobby phone and ordered the cab.

"California talk. Is neat, hey?" he said, hanging up.

"Pardon? Oh. I think it's *for* sure."

"What I said. Floor sure." He grinned. "Want to hear more? I'm knowing moch California words. In Cairo, where I come from, we are all being natural linguals. I'm knowing 'Serve up, beach baby,' and 'Good hibernations,' and—"

He broke off to answer a buzz and bring someone's car around. Then Peg's taxi came, and he helped her in.

"Night, Lady Bailey," he said. "I tell more vocabularies when you coming again."

She was glad she could keep the tears back until the door closed.

CHAPTER FIVE

"You don't sound good, dear," Ellen Bailey said. "Are you getting a cold?"

"It's seven thirty in the morning, Mother. Nobody sounds good at seven thirty in the morning."

"You usually sound better than this. Is everything all right?"

"Everything is fine." Everything is horrible. If I were on a bridge, I'd jump off.

"The weather's starting to warm up a little here. Peg? Good heavens. What's that barking?"

"It's a dog."

"I guessed that much. Is he yours?"

"Diane's," Peg said. "I'm baby-sitting. Doggy-sitting. Her name is Blondie. She's just a pup."

"That must be fun. Are your furniture and rugs surviving?"

"The rugs are okay—she's pretty well outside-trained. I'm trying to teach her to stay off the furniture, though."

"Good luck. That's not easy. Is anything else new? How did you make out with that shirt you called me about? Did the stain go away?"

Peg swallowed. "Yes."

"Well, I'll say good-bye, dear. Cheer up, will you? Nothing can be that bad."

Yes it can, Peg thought, hanging up.

"Another rum punch?" the soft island voice asked.

David sighed. "No, thanks. Just the check."

He watched the waitress walk away, her slim hips moving ever so slightly beneath her flower-print skirt. She had the kind of long, fluid shape Peg had. Her profile was a bit like Peg's, too, with its small chin and elegant cheekbones.

He picked up the paper umbrella that had come in his drink and idly twirled it. This wasn't the first time on his trip he'd seen some resemblance to Peg in a woman. It was, in fact, about the eighty-third time.

He couldn't get her off his mind.

As he found himself doing constantly, he replayed their last evening once more. He did part one first, the half that warmed him, that made him tingle with remembered pleasure. He felt again her satiny complexion, the sensuous planes of her body where he'd stroked her, his hands busy, hungry. He relived his sensation that night of drinking cool water after a long thirst, the sense of a longing just starting to be satisfied, with much more yet to come. He felt again the control he'd forced on himself. He'd tried so hard not to storm her, not to rush. There would be plenty of time.

What a laugh. If he felt like laughing, which he didn't, and wouldn't for the foreseeable future.

Which led to part two—also known as The End.

He leaned back in his wicker wing chair and looked out at the water. It was an achingly clear turquoise beneath a sky with only dots of cloud. A warm breeze, sweet with the scent of the tropics, lifted the leaves of the cashew tree above where he sat on the hotel patio. Two pelicans made arcs against the horizon, their long bills moving as they scanned the sea for their lunch.

Yet again a lovely, promising evening had been lost under an avalanche of shock. This time, too unforgivable a shock to come back from.

He'd been so outraged, he was glad to see Peg go. He knew Hassan would take care of her. For all his too-familiar eccentricity, the man took his job very seriously; he'd have carried her home piggyback if there were no cab.

Days later he'd started to miss her, as he had before, but this was worse: there was more to miss.

He'd thought and thought about what she'd done. It was such a violation of his rights, of his privacy. And keeping it a secret—letting things progress, learning about each other like any two people— when all the time she'd already—

He'd never been so humiliated.

The waitress brought his check, and he signed it and wrote his room number. She thanked him with a shy smile, put a hibiscus blossom on the table, and went away.

Of course, when Peg finally *had* told him, she'd told all. She could have said she'd seen a TV monitor; she could have claimed she'd just passed by. Mainly she could have lied about watching him. There was no need to admit that. She could have said she'd taken one look and beat feet out of there. If it had been him . . .

Well, that was the thing. He would have used one of those. But that still left the big question. Never mind what cover-up he might or might not have picked—*would he have watched in the first place?*

It was that zinger that kept him awake these exotic nights. Because despite what he'd told Peg, he couldn't kid himself: there wasn't a scrap of doubt that had he happened to spot Peg Bailey taking off her clothes where he could see her and stay hidden, he'd watch. He'd watch his damn head off.

He drained the last of his rum punch and stood.

The flight attendant had given him a news magazine in a plastic cover. They always did that; when you traveled in a suit and tie, they took you for the news magazine type. Well, he couldn't argue. He *was* the news magazine type.

He couldn't concentrate on it today, though. Just his luck that the attendant was wearing Peg's perfume. A lot of it, too. The smell was still there, even though she hadn't been past in ten minutes.

His seatmate, a man in his twenties, leaned over David to adjust his overhead light, and the smell got stronger. It was his hair. The guy's hair smelled like Peg.

He never spoke to strangers, but now, without thinking, David turned to the man.

"Excuse me," he said. "Do you mind telling me what that smell is in your hair?"

Immediately he wanted to throttle himself. If he had to ask such an idiotic thing, he could at least have made it sound like a normal question: What's that aftershave? or, Can you tell me the name of your cologne so I can get some for my brother?

"It must be the stuff I use on it," the man said, looking at him as strangely as he deserved. "It's called Vita-Gel."

"Thank you," David said stiffly.

They were a little late landing in New York, but he still had twenty minutes before his connecting flight to Hartford. David found a drugstore in the terminal and went in. They had Vita-Gel. He grabbed a tube, paid, and left.

He was standing outside the store with the opened tube in his hand when he realized what he was doing. He stayed very still for a minute. Then he put the tube back in the bag, stuffed it into a trash can, and hurried to the bank of pay phones.

The doorbell rang just as Peg was taking her chicken out. She put the pan on the counter, removed her oven mitts, and went to answer, glancing unhappily at the tumble of newspapers and couch cushions in the living room. Diane had collected Blondie just an hour ago, and she hadn't had a chance to tidy up. Well, too bad. Whoever was here could live with it.

"I called, but the line was busy," David said when she opened the door.

"David!" she shouted, her face lighting up.

His chocolate-brown suit was a bit wrinkled, but otherwise he was the same devastating man she'd so regretfully left a week before. The man she'd been sure truly wouldn't be back this time. Her heart was thumping away.

"I couldn't wait to see you," he said, his face very serious.

"That—that makes me feel wonderful," Peg said, and put her arms around him. He held her close.

She'd been so low, so lost. She'd thought of calling him, imagined the conversation, and realized she couldn't; it wouldn't do any good. He'd have treated her with cold courtesy and she'd have felt worse still. Any move would have to come from him. And the chances of that were slimmer than Blondie's whiskers.

She hugged him harder. She knew it would be all right now. She'd seen it in his face; she could feel it under her hands.

Finally they stood apart. Peg breathed deeply to stop the tears that threatened. She'd had to do that so much lately. Well, no more, it looked like. She smiled.

She stepped back and looked at him. His voice in her ear, his lovely deep voice, was wonderful to hear again; she wanted to fill her eyes with him too.

"You look a little—undone," she said. "It isn't like you."

"I just came from the airport."

"Really?" she said. "Just now?"

He nodded. "I flew in from Tortola tonight. The trip I"—he smiled slightly—"needed the bathing suit for. All the time I was away, I thought and thought about you. About what happened, everything. I was mad as hell."

He held her shoulders. "Of course I got to missing you. After a while I found myself acting like an idiot. Don't ask," he told her as she started to speak. "When it reached the point that I risked missing my plane to Hartford so I could buy some hair stuff that smelled like you, I realized I couldn't stay away. And"—he dropped his hands to her waist—"I didn't want to. Not for a second longer than it would take me to get here."

He drew her close and kissed her. Peg was engulfed by a sweet tide. Day after day, night after wakeful night, she'd pictured this—but as a joy she'd held for a moment and lost, not as something she'd have again. And now that it was back, now that *he* was back, she'd make sure not to lose him.

"David," she whispered against his mouth.

"I know, love," he said, and kissed her again, his hands strong on her back as he pressed her to him.

The phone rang. It was Diane, calling to thank her for keeping Blondie. When she hung up, David reached for her, but a steaming saucepan caught her eye.

"My broccoli," she said. "It'll cook to mush."

"Hm?"

"I was just getting dinner." She turned off the burner. "I'm glad you're here to share it—I hate to eat alone. Are you hungry?"

He looked as if he could happily keep holding and kissing her through the next eight mealtimes, but he said gamely, "I sure am." He sniffed. "What are you making?"

"Chicken."

From behind her he put his arms around her waist and kissed her neck.

"I'll never get this on the table if you don't stop that."

He moved his mouth to her ear. "Stop what?" he whispered.

She dropped her oven mitt and started to turn to him, but the phone rang again. She talked for several minutes. David went into the living room and looked out the window.

"That was my boss," she said when she'd hung up. "Trouble at the store. We've been missing some very expensive gowns, so we tightened up on security—but another one was taken anyway."

"You're not being blamed, are you?" he asked.

"Oh, no. Even Mr. Burgholtz can't stick one detective with that responsibility when there's obviously a professional at work. He was just warning me that we'll be putting in some extra hours."

She went back to the stove. "I'll have this ready in a minute," she said. "You must be wiped out. Sit down and relax."

"Sure I can't set the table or something?"

"Next time," she said, and smiled to herself. How lovely that there would *be* a next time. "Just take it easy for now. Flying is so tiring."

"I am pretty beat," he said gratefully.

A second later there was a loud *snap*. "Eeaah!" David yelled. Peg rushed in. He was standing at the newspaper-littered couch, staring at it.

"What the hell was that?" he shouted.

She looked at the couch. Then she remembered. "Oh, my God!" she said. "Blondie!"

"What are you talking about? I swear, something on here just bit me!" He pulled the newspapers off the cushions. An object underneath fell to the floor, and he picked it up.

"A mousetrap," he said wonderingly, turning it over in his hands.

"Yes," Peg said.

" 'Yes'? What do you mean, 'yes'?"

"I mean, yes, I know it's a mousetrap. I put it there." She clenched her fists. The man hadn't been here fifteen minutes, and already . . . after she'd vowed that if she ever had another chance, there wouldn't be the slightest . . .

"You put a mousetrap on the couch," he said pleasantly. "That seems to make perfect sense to you."

"Well," she said, "I was—"

"Never mind." He held up his hand. "I don't want to know." Carefully he put it back. He picked up the papers and laid them over it.

"I made up my mind," he said, sitting in a chair, "that I wasn't going to let any little glitches like this stand in the way of how I feel about you."

She was immensely relieved. "I'm glad," she said. "And I hate to find myself apologizing to you again, but—"

"No need," he said. "I'm fine."

Peg returned to the stove. She wished he'd let her explain, but if he wanted to forget it, okay. He was being flexible, that was the main thing.

She put the chicken under the broiler for a minute to reheat, then had to yank it out before it blackened. The way her hands shook, she was surprised she could get the chicken, broccoli, and salad onto the table in more or less edible condition. Having

93

David here—having him *back*—was so wonderful, she could barely walk and talk, never mind serve dinner.

She called him into the compact dining area and they sat down. She passed him dishes, feeling his eyes on her, not meeting them. She was afraid that if she looked at him, she'd leap up from the table and drape herself across his lap.

"This is delicious," David said enthusiastically.

"Thank you."

"What gives the chicken that unusual taste?"

"Onions and apricots," she said.

"Really. Well, you're a talented cook. I'm not much of one myself."

"No?" she asked politely, remembering his sludge-strong coffee.

They ate for a minute in silence. She thought of saying she'd happily cook for him anytime, or even just that he should try her lasagna, but that would sound too eager. One thing she *did* have to do, though, was clear up the matter of the mousetrap. She wanted him to see her as a more moderate, sensible person. It was too bad he'd sat on the thing, but at least it was there for a reason.

"By the way," she said, "about the mousetrap—"

"I told you. It's forgotten."

"No," Peg said, "I want to explain." She looked up from her plate and his eyes were right there, rays of heat. She made herself look down again. "I was baby-sitting for Diane's dog. Blondie's just a puppy, and she doesn't know to stay off furniture yet." Forgetting, she met his gaze again, felt the pull, swallowed, and looked out the window. "I read that if you leave a mousetrap under some newspapers and the dog jumps up, it will scare the dog without hurting it. I just forgot and left it there."

She went back to her dinner. Her plate was still quite full.

"Like I told you, no problem," David said. "It's my own fault, anyway, for dropping in."

Then he said, "Peg, look at me."

She did. His eyes searched her face, their gray depths alive with emotion. She looked at his wide sweet mouth, the little shadow beneath his lower lip where it curved. She put her fork down.

David stood, leaving his own full plate. He came around the table, took her hands, and pulled her up.

"I'm not going to wait any longer," he said. He put her arms around his neck and pressed her waist to bring her against him. He ran his hands up and down her sides, just barely touching the beginning swell of her breasts, while he covered her mouth with his.

She kissed him back with joy so intense it was almost an ache. They were really going to make love. The fantasy figure from that first day in the dressing room would at last become real.

"Come on," David said. He took her hand and led her into the bedroom. Before they were there, he was loosening his tie and unbuttoning his shirt with his other hand. Once inside, he bent to kiss her, his fingers still busy with his clothes.

"Do you have any idea," he asked, his lips brushing her ear, "how much I want you?"

She had more than an idea. She knew how he'd taken over her dreams, her thoughts, to create a fe-

95

vered need of her own. She knew. Oh, how she knew.

He was finished with his buttons. He took off his shirt and tossed it, not turning to see where it landed. Peg looked at his chest, the smooth field of golden skin with its patch of dark hair. The mounds of muscle in his arms and shoulders were just as she recalled them. Her memory was rapidly supplying the rest, the intensely masculine picture he presented without a stitch on—but her memory was the only place it had been appearing so far. She could hardly believe that he was truly here now, in front of her—that David himself was in her bedroom, half naked and wanting her.

He stroked her hair back with both hands. He kissed her eyes, then her mouth.

"You have an advantage over me," he said. "You had a preview."

Peg reddened. "I—"

"But don't worry. I'm going to even that score right away." He went to the top button of her denim blouse, saw it was a snap, and pulled the whole thing open. He took it off, his eyes on her breasts beneath her sheer white bra. Then he removed that.

Peg closed her eyes. A moment later she gasped; David's mouth was on her breasts, then his hands, his big wide hands. He groaned and pulled her to him, pressing her back to bring her bare skin to his chest.

"You're really beautiful," he said softly. "Your body, and everything about you. I love you so much. Do you love me?"

"Oh," she said, wishing she could think of some word stronger than yes.

"Do you?" he demanded.

"Yes, I do, I do," she whispered. "I've never felt anything like this."

David's hands were pushing down into the back of her jeans. She stepped back to let him get at the zipper. But he couldn't let her go just yet; he abandoned her waist and put his arms around her. His hands were a loving force on her back, on her buttocks, pulling her as close as he could.

His kisses were hungrier now. His tongue seemed to be taking possession inside her mouth, claiming every hidden corner.

Peg touched David's face, moving her fingers over it. They traced the sharp line of his jaw and lingered on his neck where the expanse of beard diminished. She stroked his shoulders and his heavy arms, feeling the muscles swell and contract as he caressed her.

His hands were at her waist, the front this time, and he stepped back a reluctant inch to have room to undo her jeans. He kissed her while he drew the zipper down.

Peg went to push the pants off her hips. David was doing it, too, and their fingers met and twined around one another as, together, they moved her jeans all the way down.

David kneeled to slip them off her feet. He pulled her onto the floor with him. She wore only her panties and he still had his slacks on, but his usual sense of logic and order was gone; his body and his feelings seemed to be doing all the thinking for him.

And he must have wanted her beneath him more than he wanted anything at that moment, because he didn't pause to finish undressing or get onto the comfortable bed right next to them. He guided Peg to the rug and moved on top of her.

The floor was hard, but Peg barely noticed. Her own thinking power was dwindling as she gave herself over to the emotions that bombarded her.

David's shoulder muscles flexed as he slid his arms underneath her back. He buried his face in her hair and kissed her neck. Then he moved a hand down to her bottom and pulled her to him there, and she thrilled to the demanding pressure.

"Peg," he whispered, "I've never wanted anyone this much."

His mouth covered hers. His kisses were hot, eager, full of need. She felt the desire building in him and it sparked a wash of longing—she wanted more of him, all there was. Blindly she pushed her hands between them and groped for his belt.

David raised his head and smiled down at her. "I guess," he said, his breathing rough, "I'm not the only one who can't wait."

Peg realized what she was doing. Shocked at herself, she yanked her hands away.

He shifted sideways. He took her hands and firmly brought them back.

"I didn't mean for you to stop," he said. "God, anything but that." She looked doubtfully at him. To make sure she got the message, he opened his belt with his left hand and used his right to put her hand on his zipper.

Peg followed his direction and pulled the zipper

down. She helped him push the slacks off and self-consciously turned away so he could remove his shorts—but wordlessly he pulled her back. Once more he guided her, and then he was nude, and he pulled her panties off so she was too.

"Now neither of us has to wait," he said.

His words of love never stopped as he moved over her once more and this time made them one. He whispered about how he felt and softly urged Peg to reveal her own emotions. She could barely get a word out; the things he said only heightened the frenzied pleasure of what he was doing, making her breathless. But she tried to obey, whispering to him of the ecstasy he was bringing her.

So many sensations at once. His lips, his hands, his strong body driving into hers. His harsh breathing, his passionate words.

He moved faster and, beyond consciousness, Peg arched to him, her lips forming sounds she was barely aware of. She was more than ready for the ultimate leap, the force that would hurl them together to the highest plateau.

With a last tug at her hips, a final push of his own, David brought her all the way. His hot whispers became an unending moan of rapture. The sound echoed through her soul as she met him, blended with him, in every way lovers can.

Presently his body cooled, but his emotions were a firestorm still. On some level he'd known for a while now that he was falling in love with Peg, but hearing himself say it had brought the reality home with a stunning jolt. Yes, he loved her; he knew it so surely, the sensation was almost an ache.

She wasn't like anyone he'd ever known. They were as unmatched as people could be. She was spacey, flaky, wacky . . . while those words barely existed in his vocabulary.

But somehow that had begun to matter less. He wanted only to hold her close, keep her with him; whatever problems their differences made, they'd work them out one way or another.

And one thing was certain: Now that they'd shared their love fully, he wasn't going to let her go no matter what.

CHAPTER SIX

David said, "Hassan's asked me three times why Lady Bailey doesn't visiting."

Peg smiled into the phone. "Tell Hassan Lady Bailey's working overtime."

"For that matter," his deep, silky voice went on, "I miss Lady Bailey myself. Keep Saturday open."

"I'm working. I'll be here till six or seven, at least."

"No problem. That leaves most of the evening—for dinner, or a movie, or"—he lowered his voice to a whisper—"a chance to find out whether my carpet is as comfortable as yours."

Peg took a deep breath.

"You didn't faint, did you?" he asked in the same soft rumble.

She chuckled. "Almost."

"Maybe," he said, "if I talk a little longer, I really can make you faint."

"I'm sure you could," she said truthfully, "but my boss would be a little upset. Oops, there's my beeper. I have to go."

"All right, love," he said. "I'll be thinking of you."

The feeling was mutual, but if she wanted to keep her job, all she could let herself think of at the moment was whatever Mr. Burgholtz was about to say. She turned on her two-way radio.

"Bailey? Go meet Carter in Children's. She needs backup on a boost. And go in easy or you'll blow it."

She swallowed her annoyance as she hurriedly put the radio back in her purse. Whatever shoplifting was going on in Children's must be significant, or Darcy Carter could handle it alone.

She went quickly up to the third floor, then slowed as she neared Children's. She strolled casually around the racks and carousels of tiny outfits, pretending to be a young mother shopping for her baby. Finally she spotted Darcy. She waited for the tall large-boned blonde to approach or signal her.

Darcy came right over. "Zip," she told Peg disgustedly. "I couldn't do a thing. They got nervous and put the stuff back."

"They?"

"Two middle-aged types with big canvas tote bags. They each put several things in them, including those sterling silver music boxes," Darcy said, pointing to a display. "But I tipped them somehow. They put the stuff back and left the floor."

"Don't blame yourself," Peg said. "They sound very experienced. You didn't have to do anything to tip them. It was probably their radar."

Darcy chuckled without humor. "Try telling that to Mr. Burgholtz."

"Well," Peg said, "you can't reason with a cement wall. He gets mad if things don't go the way he wants and just takes out his frustration on the nearest target. He's been giving everyone in Women's an even harder time than usual since those gowns started going."

"True enough," Darcy said. "Are we making any progress at all?"

"No. A bunch of us are on overtime every night, and the gowns are still marching out of here." She stopped talking for a minute as a customer paused near them to look through some sweaters. "Two last week," she said. "A total of four thousand retail."

"Incredible. Listen, we'd better break this up. I'll see you later."

"Right," Peg said. "Call me if you see the tote-bag ladies at it again."

She went back down to Women's. The long hours were getting to her; she was tired, and the others working on the thefts looked it too. Morale was down. Teamwork would help, but Hugh Burgholtz's small-mindedness discouraged that. He put down the detectives' efforts and ridiculed any suspicion not backed with proof.

It was a shame, really. All he succeeded in doing was guaranteeing that he never heard his employees' good ideas. Why should people share their observations if the boss was too foolish to consider them?

She checked with Betty Henry, determinedly ignoring the direction her imagination fought to take as she walked through the fitting room area and made her rounds, working her way over to Coats. Just as she got there, her beeper sounded.

She thought fast. She was too far from any of the fitting rooms or offices to duck into one to use her radio. Ordinarily she could afford the time to get there, but if Darcy needed her, every instant counted.

There was no question of taking the radio out without cover. That was strictly forbidden for all detectives; they couldn't do their jobs without their anonymity.

So she had no privacy. Well, she'd better create some, now. Quickly she crawled behind a row of full-length coats on a wall rack and took out her radio, turning the volume way down.

"Bailey?" Mr. Burgholtz said. "What happened with Carter?"

"Nothing," she whispered. She shifted her head to push an angora muffler out of her eyes, and got a lapel in her mouth. "Ugh," she said, feeling the wool fibers on her tongue.

"What, Bailey? I can't hear you. Where the hell are you?"

"In Coats," she said, wishing she weren't in them quite so literally. She raised her hand to pick the fibers out of her mouth, then changed her mind and put it back down. That much motion would show. All she needed was for some customer to start wondering why the coats were moving.

"Well, what about Carter's case?" he demanded.

"Flmph," she said.

"*What?*"

Her mouth was full of angora hairs. Every time she opened it to try to work them out with her tongue, more came in. She couldn't speak audibly with the stuff in there, and she couldn't remove it without—

She froze. She couldn't see, but she knew a customer was close; she heard breathing, and she felt the slight movement of the coats as the person looked them over.

Even though there was nothing she wanted more passionately at this moment than to spit, Peg closed her mouth resignedly and concentrated on staying still. Her tongue felt like a rabbit had sat on it, and she had tension aches in muscles she hadn't known she possessed, but she flattened herself against the wall behind the coats, pressed the button that silenced the radio, and tried not to breathe.

Go away, she silently implored the customer. Shop somewhere else, like in Budapest. You don't need a coat. Even if you do, you don't want *these* coats. They get near your mouth and it's like you took a bite out of one. Wouldn't you rather have a nice lightweight down-filled—

The woman was coming closer. Peg felt more movement as she slowly examined coats that must have been only a couple of feet away.

Leave! she screamed noiselessly. You just remembered a dental appointment. You just found out your house is on fire.

The wool swished right near her face. Her heart hammered. She tried to calm herself. With any luck the woman would walk away now; Peg was at the end of the rack, so there were no more coats to look at. Even if she touched every single one, they were bulky enough to keep Peg hidden, as long as the woman didn't take one off the hanger.

She held her breath. It would be over in a second.

But it wasn't over. A hanger clanged as a coat was

removed, and suddenly Peg was staring into the horror-struck face of a small white-haired woman in her seventies.

The woman screamed and jumped away. Peg jammed her radio into the nearest coat pocket and pushed her way out, swiping hairs from her mouth.

"It's all right," she soothed the woman. "I work here. I was just, uh, checking the tickets on the coats. I didn't mean to scare you."

"Well, good heavens," the woman gasped, her hand at her chest.

A saleslady came over to see what the fuss was. "Mrs. Musselman, is something wrong?" she asked anxiously. "Are you ill?"

"Ill with fright," the woman said. "I've never been so shocked in my life."

"But what happened?" the saleslady asked, looking from the customer to Peg.

Peg said, "It's hard to explain. I—"

"Bailey! What in hell's sweet name is going on?" Hugh Burgholtz thundered from twenty feet away. "Do you know how much of my time you're wasting? What kind of scene have you got going now?"

Peg glared. "Which question would you like me to answer first?" she asked tightly.

"Are you in charge?" the customer asked him. "Because this young woman gave me the most awful fright. I was looking through the wool coats when suddenly—"

"Later," Burgholtz said with a dismissive wave. "Bailey, I asked what—"

"Mr. Burgholtz," the saleswoman interrupted,

"Mrs. Musselman is a Smith-Clove customer of long standing. *Very* long standing."

"What? Oh," the balding man said. "Oh." He scratched his head. "Ma'am, why don't you put your statement in a letter? I'll consider it very carefully. Bailey, come to the office."

He started off, glancing back to make sure Peg followed.

"Wait," the customer called. "To whose attention should I send the letter?"

"Mine," Burgholtz answered shortly, his supply of courtesy depleted.

"But what is your—"

"I'll write it down for you, Mrs. Musselman," the saleslady said. She put her arm around the frail woman and led her to a chair.

Hugh Burgholtz slammed the office door. "All right," he said. "What *was* that circus all about?"

Peg knew she had no reason to feel defensive, but unconventional decisions weren't popular with the security director. There was no way she could explain the situation and not have it sound like a Muppets movie.

She gave it a go anyway. "When my beeper went off," she began, "I wasn't near a place where I could use the radio. So I—"

"What do you mean, you weren't near a place? You could have walked over to—"

"I didn't want to take the *time*," Peg said doggedly. "I thought Darcy might be calling me back to help with her case."

His own beeper sounded, and he took his radio out of his jacket and spoke into it. When he was finished, he held out his hand. "Let me see yours. Something went wrong with it while I was talking to you."

"Nothing was wrong," she said, opening her handbag to get it. "I just—"

"I'll decide that," he said, wiggling his hand impatiently.

The radio wasn't there. "Oh, hell," she said remembering.

"Now what?"

"I left it in—in Coats."

"What?" he shouted. "You lost it?"

"No! It's in the pocket of a coat on the rack."

"In the pocket of a coat," he repeated disgustedly.

"I stuck it there so the customer wouldn't see it. You're always telling us to keep a low profile."

"But you're not supposed to stash your gear in the merchandise, Bailey!"

"I had no choice! The customer would have seen me put it back in my bag."

"I think," he said, leaning back in his chair, "it's time you told me exactly what happened. The whole thing. Quit giving me pieces."

"I've been *trying* to tell you. You keep interrupting."

He waved that away. "Just talk. Let's hear it."

She explained what had happened with Darcy's case. "Then," she went on, "I was beeped over in Coats, and I thought Darcy might need me fast. Since I didn't want to risk losing those people she was watching," Peg said, knowing it was futile to try to convince him she'd made a good decision but damned if she wouldn't try anyway, "I hid behind a rack to use the radio. Of course, it was you. Then I heard that woman going through the coats, and I shut up. There's nothing wrong with the radio."

"And how come you couldn't put it in your bag again?"

"The customer would have seen it."

"How could she see your radio if you were hidden?"

"I—wasn't hidden at that point."

Burgholtz gaped at her. "You walked out of a rack of coats in front of a customer?"

"I did, yes. After I'd—been discovered."

Once again he sat back in his chair, his low brow creased as he tried to follow. Finally he said, "No. Tell me it didn't happen that way."

"What way?" she asked unnecessarily.

"The old lady caught you in there, didn't she?"

"Yes," Peg said with as much dignity as she could counterfeit.

"What a disaster," he said with awe. "The woman is going through the coats—here's a red one, here's a brown one, here's a green one—and suddenly here's Bailey's face, popping out at her like a Halloween skeleton. Good God. No wonder the old broad looked like she was having a coronary."

"If you're finished," Peg said, getting up, "I'll go get my radio now."

"Do that. And while you're at it, see if you can get yourself some *brains!* That old lady is a good customer!"

"I know she is," Peg said, pausing at the door. "I

was there when you found out. At least *I* only scared the woman. *You* treated her like a bag lady!"

"*Out!*" he roared as she banged the door shut.

Hassan opened Peg's car door. "Long time no see-ing." A grin lit up his dark, smooth face. "You come to visiting Mr. Robertson this cold Saturday evening?"

"Just for a few minutes. Then we're going to dinner."

Hassan nodded his approval. "Your dress is liking me," he said.

"Liking?"

"You know." He waved his hands. "Happying."

"Pleasing?" Peg suggested.

"*Pleasing.* Yes. What that color is calling? Sound like baby dogs, isn't it?"

Peg frowned, trying to understand. "I'm not sure what you mean. The color is called lavender." He looked blank. "Some people call it mauve. Or purple."

"Purple! Yes," he said. "Purpies. Baby dogs." He winked proudly as he got into her car. "Is why I'm knowing moch vocabularies. I make connections. My memory secret." He tapped his head and screeched off.

Peg rode to David's floor, chuckling to herself. He welcomed her in with a grin that telegraphed how glad he was to see her and immediately pulled her into a hug and pressed her cheek to his.

"Miss me?" he asked.

She nodded, realized she was probably scraping his face with the extra gel she'd put on her hair to

110

rescue it after her long day, and hugged him tighter instead. He kissed her ear and stepped back.

"I have a present for you," he said.

"A present?"

He nodded. "Just a little something to cheer you up. After your rotten experience with that slimeball you work for, I thought you could use a treat. Not that I didn't see his point, even if he is a slimeball. A security director is an administrator, and an administrator can't let his staff go around doing crazy things."

"You told me."

"There are more conventional ways to handle tight situations like the one you were in, and you can't blame Burgholtz for expecting you to use one. Hiding behind a bunch of coats is hardly the—"

She sighed. "So you said."

"Sorry. I guess I've made my point. I'll get the present."

She kissed him. "I can't wait."

"Just consider it my way of helping out," he said, going into the bedroom. "You told me you were planning to get this, but with the hours you've been putting in you can't have had time. So I did it for you."

Peg waited, curious and excited, thinking that the present she was most interested in was David himself, so sexy in his gray pinstripe suit. As always, his body seemed to send an aura through his clothes, as if he were dressed and nude at the same time. And as always, she couldn't look at him without seeing him as she first had and feeling the charge inside she'd felt then. But it was even more electric now that she knew not only what his body looked like but what it felt like beside her, above her, within her. . . .

"Here you go, love," David said. He handed her a big box tied with a white bow.

She gazed at it in delighted suspense.

"Open it," he said.

She untied the ribbon, lifted the lid, and found several layers of white tissue. Eagerly she pushed them aside and took out her gift. Her jaw dropped.

"Oh, David," she said.

He stood with his arms folded, beaming. "Like it?"

"I—I'm speechless," she answered honestly. The coat was truly the most hideous thing she'd ever seen. The yellow wasn't yellow; it was closer to chartreuse—the color they put on monster masks to make them glow in the dark. The color of Gatorade.

For a wildly hopeful moment she wondered if it was just a trick of the light. Maybe the color wasn't so bad. Casually she moved away from the lamp to the other end of the couch, where she'd dropped her own coat, and held the new one near it to see if it looked any better.

It looked even worse. The buttery shade of her old coat still showed through the grime, making the new one look more bilious yet.

"Put it on," David said eagerly. "See if it fits."

Fit! She'd forgotten about that! Holding her breath, praying, Peg fumbled for the tag—and had to suppress a cheer. It was an eight; she wore at least a ten in a coat.

"Oh!" she said. "I mean—oh, dear. It's too small."

"I don't think so." He took it and held it for her to put on.

"It is, definitely. I never wear an eight." But her relief was turning to chagrin as the coat settled on her slim frame as if its tailor had measured every inch of her.

"The saleswoman insisted this style ran very big," David said. He turned her to face him. "She was right! It's a perfect fit."

"How—how do you like it on me?" Peg asked, turning to show him every angle. Please, she prayed, see how it really looks. Use that fabulous taste of yours and realize that in this color I look like a corpse. Say to me, "You know what, Peg? I've changed my mind. That's not the coat for you. I must have been temporarily blind when I bought it."

"You know what, Peg?" he said.

Her heart leapt. "What?"

"It looks absolutely stunning on you."

No, she thought, it doesn't. It looks like somebody's face just before they're seasick.

"I'm really going to enjoy seeing you wear it."

No, you're not. You aren't going to see me do anything, because as soon as I get home I'm hanging myself.

"I'll cut off the tags so you can put it on for tonight."

Leave them. They'll distract people's attention.

"By the way," he said, "you won't believe this, but I was a little nervous about choosing this coat." Not noticing Peg's strangled cough, he went on. "I know what *I* like in clothes, of course, but I wasn't

113

sure if I could pick something wild enough for you. So I decided I considered it a challenge. And when I saw that baby, and it looked awfully bright to me, I said to myself, 'Loosen up, Robertson—you're a stick. Nothing's too bright for Peg.' " He grinned. "Right?"

She nodded, not trusting her mouth to produce an affirmative word.

"Well," he said briskly, "let's put your old one in the incinerator right now."

Peg gasped. "In the *incinerator?*"

"Sure. Why keep it around if it's been replaced?"

"But—I've never heard of such a thing! Who would put a coat in the incinerator?"

He scooped it up. "If more people got rid of their old clothes, they wouldn't have overstuffed closets. It's the sensible way."

"But, David, you can't—" She had to save her poor coat. "I mean—"

He looked questioningly at her.

"It's—it's too bulky for the incinerator. It'll clog it."

"Not a chance," he said. "This building is a fortress. You could put a house trailer down that incinerator." He started for the door.

"Wait!" Peg said.

He stopped. She hadn't the slightest idea what she was going to say.

"Um," she began.

He waited.

"Could—could I have a glass of water?"

"Sure, in a second. I'll be right back—the incinerator's next door."

"But listen—I just remembered. You can't throw the coat out. My mother wants it."

"Your mother?" He looked confused. "Didn't you mention that she's five feet tall?"

"Oh," Peg improvised, "I didn't mean she wants to *wear* it. Good grief. The very idea." She laughed, a little hysterically. "She wants to use it for—for—"

He nodded encouragingly.

"Quilting," she finished desperately.

"Really," David said, handing her the coat. "That's intriguing to a city guy. How do they do it?"

"It's easy," she said with an offhand wave. She actually couldn't begin to imagine how they did it. She'd grown up in an apartment building in the city of Louisville, Kentucky and had never even seen a handmade quilt. She bet her mother hadn't, either.

"Tell me about it," David said, joining her on the couch. "I'm interested in the mechanics. Oh, sorry, I forgot your water." He went to the kitchen and came back with a glass.

Peg sipped it, wondering how long one could avoid explaining something by constantly having a mouthful of water. She was down to the last half inch when, thank goodness, the house phone rang and David went to get it.

"That was Hassan," he said. He looked at his watch. "We were so busy with the coat I forgot the time. I asked him to have the car ready at eight thirty, and it's twenty of nine."

They went downstairs. Hassan opened the door for them.

"Lady Bailey, Mr. Robertson." He smiled. "This

115

is being my lucky day. Two beautiful ladies, one after the other following." He gestured toward a striking honey-skinned brunette pulling away in a late-model Ford.

Peg looked over. "I'm sure I know her," she said. "What's her name?"

"Is Lady Hewitt," Hassan said. He pronounced it "Hayweet," but the right name clicked in just before he spoke, because Peg remembered who the woman was. Shirley Hewitt worked on the cleaning crew at Smith-Clove, arriving, as all the cleaners did, about when Peg was leaving.

"You are knowing Lady Hewitt?" Hassan asked. Just then he noticed her new coat. His thick eyebrows went up. "Lady Bailey," he began, shaking his head, "you are so lovely, so nice dressing always, I must advice you—this coat—"

Peg saw with horror that he was about to speak the truth about the nightmare she was wearing, right in front of David.

"You're right," she said quickly, "it doesn't go with my dress. But that's because—"

"You no understanding. I say this coat—"

"—doesn't match my purple dress. That's true, it doesn't. But that's because Mr. Robertson bought it for me without knowing I had this dress on."

"Wait." Hassan held up his hand. He was clearly determined to be understood. "What I meaning—"

"I *know*," Peg said, looking hard at Hassan, praying *he'd* understand. "But Mr. Robertson had no idea what dress I was wearing *when he gave me this coat for a present.*"

Hassan studied her, frowning. She risked a glance

at David, saw he was looking away, and put a finger to her lips.

It worked. Hassan's face brightened.

"Ah, yes," he said loudly. "Like I am remarking, this is moch excellent coat." He gave Peg a big wink. "Floor sure."

"Let's go," David said, taking Peg's hand. "Our reservation is for nine."

They got into the car. As Hassan closed Peg's door, he said, "You want I'm giving Lady Hewitt hello for you?"

"Sure," Peg said. "Next time she comes to work here, tell her Peg Bailey said hi. Peg Bailey from Smith-Clove."

Hassan looked puzzled. "Work?"

"She cleans for someone in the building, doesn't she?"

He shrugged. "I only know here is her living house. Twenty-two J."

They drove out to the street. Peg asked David, "How fluent is your Hassan-ese? Did he mean Shirley Hewitt lives there?"

"I think so."

"Isn't that something," she said. "I must be in the wrong line of work. Do cleaning people have a powerful union? Even a studio in your building must cost as much as a yacht."

"There aren't any studios in the building. Anyway, didn't Hassan say twenty-two J? The J units are the biggest." He put his arm around her and moved his fingers up under her hair to stroke her neck. "But my unit is an H. And the H," he said in a low whisper, "has the softest, thickest carpeting."

They stopped at a light, and he leaned over and nipped her chin. "The kind that feels great under your bare back."

Peg's mind was still on Shirley Hewitt and the provocative question of how a cleaning person could afford a huge, beautiful apartment in one of the priciest high rises in town. Her detective antennae were quivering madly; a gap between a Smith-Clove worker's earnings and expenditures was something she was trained to check out. As soon as she got back to the store, she'd do just that.

But as David moved around to her ear, she closed her eyes and forgot everything but the moist warmth of his tongue, his delicious scent . . . and the promises his busy hands were making for later.

CHAPTER SEVEN

"Did you wear heavy socks over your regular ones?" David asked. "Good. Pull them up over your jeans."

He watched Peg struggle to do it.

"Wait," he said. "Let me." He fixed her socks, then showed her how the shoes fitted into the snap closures of the cross-country skis. He checked to see that she'd done it right, then put his skis on. He helped her stand.

"You're all set," he said. "How do you feel?"

"Like a newborn colt. Am I actually supposed to move on these things without collapsing backward?"

"Don't worry." He took her hand. "You'll be buzzing along like a pro before you know it."

"That," Peg said, moving one ski a shaky few inches, "is what people always tell you when the truth is too depressing."

"Trust me. Cross-country is the best type of skiing for people who don't ski. No lift, no heights, no boots, no windburn—"

"And no *fun*," she complained. "I thought the whole point of skiing was what you do after it." She waved at the little woodstove-heated trailer where

119

they'd rented their gear. "That's not my idea of après-ski. Where does the hot buttered rum come in?"

"Just sort of slide your feet," David said. "Don't try to walk. Listen, I wanted to take you away for a weekend in Vermont, remember? Snow-covered chalet and the whole enchilada. You were the one who couldn't take the time off."

"True."

"We're lucky to still *have* snow in Connecticut in March."

"Also true." She pushed forward the way he'd shown her, gathered courage, and went a little farther. "What really makes me mad is that I'll bet my hat Shirley Hewitt will turn out to be the reason I'm putting in all these hours. And you can bet *she*'s having a nice weekend. Maybe at one of those snow-covered chalets—the most expensive one. And drinking *my* hot buttered rum."

"Use your poles. No, try to coordinate them with your feet. That's it. You're doing great. Only a little farther to the tracks, and then you'll really get into it."

Peg tucked a wisp of hair under her wool cap with a mittened hand. "I keep thinking I'm going to fall."

"You are. You're going to fall a lot. Why do you think I made you wear all that underwear? For insulation, but for padding too."

"That's not very encouraging," she grumbled.

David leaned over and kissed her forehead, then resumed his ski stance with perfect grace. "I'll pick you up."

She grinned at him. It was fun to watch him, the way his strong legs slid rhythmically along the snow, but she quickly learned she couldn't look sideways and stay upright too. Reluctantly she shifted her attention to the scene ahead of them.

She had to admit it was beautiful. They were entering a pine forest that was barely disturbed except for the machine-pressed ski tracks and occasional animal prints. The tracks made a narrow double path that wound through the woods, up and down gentle hills, along a dark clear brook. As David had promised, her skis fit snugly into the grooves, making movement much easier.

"So," David said, sliding along in front of her, his poles making measured *thunks*, "you think she's the one? The cleaning woman?"

"Yes. She has no police record, and I can't prove anything—at least I can't yet. But I have a strong hunch about her. I've poked around, and she doesn't seem to have any means of support besides the cleaning work—yet she rents that apartment. She's aloof and unfriendly at the store, and keeps to herself. Plus, it just fits; gowns are the kind of thing someone like Hewitt would take. I just don't know how she's getting them out of the store. The cleaning people are searched when they leave."

"And you're still not going to tell your boss about her? I don't think that's wise."

Peg started to answer and lost her poling rhythm. She yelled to David, but when he turned she'd managed to keep from toppling.

"Good!" he said. "You're getting the hang of it."

"I am?"

121

"Sure. Isn't it easier?"

"Yes," she admitted, surprised. She was putting one foot in front of the other and actually skiing—she whose athletic aptitude was limited to turning on an occasional Red Sox game.

"Anyway, I'm not telling Mr. Burgholtz. The way he looks at it, I have nothing to tell."

"But that's not good business procedure," David argued. "The chain of command is there for a reason."

"You don't understand. My boss likes nice, neat packages. Here's the culprit, there's the lock pick in his hand. He doesn't want to hear suspicions—especially not from me. He's always accusing me of—a lack of caution."

"With good reason, it sounds like."

"David—"

"I'm just being honest," he said, glancing back. "From things you tell me that happen at the store, and from what I see, I have to agree with Burgholtz. You tend to be too impulsive and make rash judgments. You get into a lot of touchy situations because of that."

"I don't want to hear this again. Especially now, when it's all I can do to stay vertical."

He decided to drop it for the moment. He did worry about her, dealing with thieves and what-not in her unorthodox ways, but there wasn't much he could do besides keep trying to talk sense into her, and this wasn't the time. He had a feeling he was starting to get through, though. Pretty soon he'd see some changes in her cowgirl style.

They skied on. Sunlight through the pine

branches made shifting patches on the snow, and the forest air was fragrant. Peg breathed in deeply. David stayed reassuringly close, leading the way but never far ahead.

"This is fun," she said.

David laughed. His breath made a white cloud. "You sound astonished."

"I am. I'm just not the athletic type."

"I don't know," he said, turning to grin devilishly at her. "Some sports you do wonderfully."

"Oh," she said, and felt her face heat up. She couldn't think of a witty comeback; she was too busy trying to ski casually along in spite of the quivery sensation washing over her.

She heard someone clear his throat behind her and, startled, she turned. A man and woman were approaching fast. They moved in swift, practiced strokes and wore matching red outfits. Peg registered all that in the instant before she lost her footing and went tumbling off the track in a tangle of skis, poles, and wool.

David scrambled to help her.

"Excuse us," the other man called haughtily as he and his partner skied on.

"Learn some courtesy, you jerk!" David yelled. He pulled Peg up, brushing off snow. He collected her poles and replaced a dislodged ski.

"Thanks," Peg said. "I'm so embarrassed."

"No way," David said. "Those two are the type cross-country skiers hate to have on the trails. Don't blame yourself. Wait a second—use a cross step to get back to the track. Like this—watch me."

Following as David criss-crossed his skis to avoid

sliding downward, Peg made her way back to the trail. "But it's humiliating. I feel like a clown, spilling over in front of people."

Suddenly David burst out laughing.

"Oh, thanks," Peg said, hurt.

"I'm not laughing at you, exactly," he said, trying to stop. "It just hit me that it's about the hell time *you* were the one to complain about being embarrassed."

"Yes, well, I guess you've had more than your share of bad moments."

"Thanks to you."

"So I'd better be a good sport, huh?"

"Absolutely. But ungrit your teeth, or I might think you don't mean it."

He glanced back to smile. Peg smiled, too, and they glided on through their green-and-white domain.

Her legs felt as if they'd never stop hurting, but she *had* had a great time. And she hadn't missed out on the hot buttered rum after all.

"I've never tasted this," Peg said, lifting her glass mug and taking a sip. It was sweet and tart at once, with a bite of cinnamon, and instantly warming.

"What do you think?" David asked.

"As good as I imagined."

She looked out the window of the roadside inn. The snow-covered trees were travelog-pretty. Finches pecked at seed some thoughtful person had scattered; occasionally they squabbled in a blur of red and brown.

"Well, I wanted you to get the rest of the package.

124

You're right—putting in the effort to ski entitles you to the after part. I'm glad we found this place. It would be nice to spend the night here."

Peg sighed. It sure would. But she had to be at work at eight tomorrow morning, and she'd never make it from here. They were ninety minutes from Hartford.

"Can I have a rain check?" she asked, pulling her ski jacket around her shoulders as a gust of wind rattled the window. Another good thing about going skiing—she'd had a day off from the Technicolor Gatorade coat she'd been faithfully wearing.

"You can have a whole book of them. I just hope you get to cash them in soon." He cut a piece of Cheddar cheese from the wedge on the table, put it on french bread, gave it to Peg, and cut one for himself. "What are you going to do next about Shirley Hewitt?"

"Watch her. It's the only way."

"If you told Burgholtz what you think," David said, "isn't it at least possible he'd assign some people to help you do that?"

Peg shook her head. "It's not only impossible, it's ludicrous. He'd no more assign personnel to check out a hunch of mine than he'd put on one of those gowns and model it."

"But how can you do it without working around the clock? You're at the store full-time plus. You can't spend all your time off following her."

"I don't have to," Peg said. She took the orange slice from her mug and bit into it. "I just need to get a bead on her routine. Then I'll be closer to the

125

answer, and I'll try for some proof to take to my boss."

"Interesting," David said. "You learn how she thinks, is that it?"

"Pretty much."

"How, exactly? How do you get into her routine and psych her out?"

"Several ways," Peg said. "Tail her on a spot-check basis. See who she talks to. Watch her car use. See where she goes, and bump into her accidentally-on-purpose—though I wouldn't do that with Shirley, since she knows who I am. Mostly I just watch and think. If you let your mind go where it wants, you'll be surprised where it takes you."

David was looking at her in an odd way, as if an idea had just struck him. He picked up his mug, then put it down without drinking from it.

He asked, "Is that what you did with me?"

Peg didn't know what he meant, and she suspected she wasn't going to like finding out. "Excuse me?" she said.

"When you came into the deli near my office. Was that 'accidentally-on-purpose'?"

She didn't answer, but the flush on her cheeks did.

"You're kidding me," he said angrily.

"No." She looked down at the table.

"For God's sake. What the hell is the matter with you?"

She said, "I thought you were flattered. You told me—"

"I'm not flattered if there was a whole damn *plot*. When will you cut this stuff out? You're always creating some scene I can't get out of without putting on a public sideshow."

Stung, Peg reacted defensively. "Maybe," she said, "you're just too self-conscious."

"What?"

"You embarrass too easily, David. You get mortified over things most people would take in stride."

"Is that so?" His voice rose; he seemed in imminent danger of embarrassing himself with no help from her. But he saw heads turning, so he lowered his voice. "Most people would *take in stride* the things you do? The things you put me through? Having their clothing dissolve in a restaurant? Being spied on while they undress in a department store? Most people would be unruffled if someone—"

"All right," Peg said, "maybe they'd be a little upset. But you—"

"They wouldn't be *a little upset*—they'd be ripped! You'd be lucky if they just sued you and didn't come after you with a posse!"

"Well," she said, "I know I'm a bit careless sometimes, but—"

"Careless? You're a walking disaster! How many more surprises have you got up your sleeve? How many other secrets will I have to pull out of you before I know every infantile, misguided, humiliating—"

"None," Peg replied angrily. She shoved back her chair and stood. "You know everything. I guess we're just not meant for each other. I'd like to go home now."

"You got it," he said, throwing some money onto the table and striding out after her.

Hassan opened the car door for him with obvious disappointment. "Lady Bailey doesn't visiting?"

"No," David said shortly.

"You have spit?"

David frowned. "What?"

"Spit. Queeble. What you call, hmm, fight."

"Oh." He was in no mood for this. "I don't care to discuss it, if you don't mind." He gave the keys to Hassan, who plainly did mind, and went to the elevator.

David was damned if he knew what to do now. He didn't even know what to *think*. A terrific day, spent doing something he loved with the most interesting woman he'd ever met. Then she ruins everything by tossing yet another bombshell at him.

He unlocked his door. It was really getting to him, the constant suspense of wondering what sideshow he'd find himself in the middle of next—or, worse, what he'd *been* in and hadn't known. Every time he started to think Peg was cleaning up her act, some new secret came out.

He poured wine, sat on the couch, and turned the TV to channel eight with the remote selector. Al Terzi was introducing the Accu-Weather forecast. It told him what he could see from his twentieth-floor window: that the night was clear and cold, with few clouds.

David wondered what the Accu-Weather people would advise about a certain lady who was driving him nuts. Even they wouldn't be able to predict the unpredictable Peg Bailey, he bet.

When the news was over, he realized he was hungry. He'd planned to have dinner with Peg in ski country. So far his anger had kept his appetite in the background, but now his stomach was asserting itself.

He went into the kitchen and took some minute steaks from the freezer.

"Lady Bailey!" Hassan said delightedly.

Peg got out of her car. "How are you, Hassan?"

"Before, I am depressing. Mr. Robertson isn't bringing you tonight. But now you are coming, so I am being groovy."

"Thank you," Peg said. "I'm glad someone's happy to see me."

"Ah," Hassan said, showing his enormous collection of gleaming teeth as he climbed into her car. "You do have spit."

"Excuse me?"

He winked. "You fight, yes? But you here to feex. You smart lady. Hang out there."

Peg went to the elevator. Hassan was pretty smart himself—she had indeed decided to "hang out there." She'd put too much into what she and David were building to let this setback be any more than that.

Still, this wasn't easy.

The elevator opened. She took a deep breath, slowly let it out, and walked to David's apartment. She pressed the bell.

Three things happened at once. David opened the

129

door; an acrid gray cloud stung her eyes and nose; and a deafening screech, like five hundred fingernails on a hundred blackboards, sounded right over her head.

He pulled her inside and shut the door. "Sorry about that."

"I can't hear you."

"Take your hands away from your ears."

"What?"

He pulled her hands down.

"That thing is still screaming," Peg said. "What *is* it?"

"Smoke alarm."

"Good grief. Is there a fire? The smoke is really heavy."

"Nah," David said. "It's just my steaks."

"Shouldn't you phone your neighbors?" Peg asked. She started to unbutton her coat, but stopped. He hadn't exactly welcomed her in; he might not want her to stay. "Won't they think it's a real fire?"

"They're used to it," he said. He stepped closer and gripped her shoulders. "Did I tell you how happy I am to see you?"

"No," she said, relief warming her.

He bent and kissed her cheek, then her mouth. His lips were a thrilling pressure.

"I know I get impatient and hot under the collar over some of the things you do," he said softly, "but it's hard not to. You have to admit, you're full of surprises—and not always nice ones." He kissed her again, then once more. This time he lingered a long minute, his tongue teasing. "I'm really glad you're here, though. I mean it."

"You do?"

"Damn right."

"I hoped you would be," Peg said. She took off the Gatorade coat and laid it on the couch. She fluffed the curls she'd tried to revive, and shuddered at her sticky fingers. "And the truth is, I have an ulterior motive."

"Well," David said, taking her hand and leading her to the kitchen, "I hope it's dinner, because there's enough for two. I'd love to have you eat with me."

Peg looked at the broiling pan on the counter. It contained several curled black things about the size of children's mittens. They looked as appetizing as mittens, too.

"No, thanks," she said. "I had dinner."

"Then maybe just some salad, to keep me company?"

"Well, okay," she said. "That would be nice."

He settled her at the dining counter. She was really stiff now; she had to lift one thigh with her hands to cross her legs.

He brought in his plate and a bowl of salad for her. She was so hungry that she'd wolfed several bites before she realized it was horrible. She didn't think you could ruin salad, but David had managed. The cucumbers and onions were cut in pieces a rhinoceros would find large. The greens had been washed but not drained, leaving the bowl full of water that diluted the dressing. Which actually wasn't such a problem, since the dressing tasted like garlicky paint thinner.

"Good?" David asked.

"Mmm," Peg said, surreptitiously washing off a cucumber log in the pool at the bottom of the bowl.

"So," he said, "if your ulterior motive wasn't dinner, what was it?"

"I was hoping you'd do a little job with me."

"What kind?" he asked.

"A stakeout. A tiny one," she added quickly as his face began to arrange itself in the familiar don't-get-me-involved look. "Sit in the car with me outside the store while I . . . observe the cleaning people leaving."

There. She'd made it sound like the legitimate work it was, with no words to scare him off, like "sneak" or "hide" or "spying."

But David was shaking his head. "I don't like the sound of that at all."

"It's nothing," she said. "Just the most routine, boring type of procedure."

"First of all," he said, "nothing you're involved in is routine and boring. Or if it is, it doesn't stay that way for long. Second, I'm not sure I want *you* hanging around watching criminals—or suspected criminals—with or without me." He cut into his last steak.

"That's my job, David."

"Still—"

"Please give me some credit," she said, putting her fork down. "I'm not a complete dingbat. I happen to be good at my work. You talk as if you think I can't do anything right."

"I don't think that. But you do take chances, you know, and I worry about you."

"You worry about my going on a stakeout?"

"Sure," he said.

"Then," she asked innocently, "wouldn't you *prefer* to be with me?"

He closed his eyes in resignation. "What exactly would this entail?"

"Very little. Like I said, I need to observe the cleaning people as they leave."

"Just observe? No funny stuff?"

"Absolutely not. I only want company. I called one of the other detectives, but she's out of town for two days, and I'd like to do it tomorrow."

"So I'm your second choice."

Peg smiled. "Only for a stakeout."

"Ask me another," David said.

"Let's see . . . the Wabash."

"Four hundred seventy-five miles."

"That's incredible," Peg said. "You really know every river in the world?"

He shrugged. "Keep trying. You might stump me."

"Ssh. Here we go. They're starting to come out. Good, the door's propped open." She lifted her binoculars.

"Why is that good?"

"Because I can see how they're being processed out. What gets searched. Keep your eyes open for Shirley Hewitt."

They watched from the car as the cleaning people trickled out to the staff parking lot.

"Are they all store employees?" David asked.

"No, none of them is. About three-quarters come from one cleaning service that Smith-Clove hires; the rest are independents. They work free-lance for the store, and for other places, and they bring their own equipment. But they all have to start work and finish at the same time, for obvious security reasons."

"Is that Hewitt? About five people back, in the green shirt and jeans."

Peg moved the binoculars. It was David's neighbor, all right, filing toward the door checkpoint with the others. She carried a large shoulder bag, and she was pulling along an upright vacuum cleaner and a long zippered bag.

Peg watched through the glasses as Hewitt's turn came. The security guard opened both bags and rummaged through them; there were brushes, brooms, rags, and a mop in the long one. He closed them, and Hewitt came out.

"She's an independent?" David asked.

"Yes. Okay, let's see which car is hers. I'm guessing she's smart enough not to drive the Ford to work."

"It's not very flashy," David said.

"No, but it's a step above what most of these people have. I'll bet she likes to keep work and home very separate."

Sure enough, the dark-haired woman went around to the back of a dented old Dodge van.

"How come they're all parked front-out?" David asked. "It's harder to load and unload that way."

"Yes, but the exit jams up so, they have to. They'd never get out otherwise."

Hewitt pulled open the van doors and lifted her things inside, giving Peg a clear view. Then she closed them and went around to the driver's seat, which was in its own cab separate from the rest of the van.

"What now?" David asked.

"Now," Peg said, starting her engine at the moment Hewitt started hers, "we follow from a ways back and see if she does what I think she will."

"Wait a minute. I only agreed to sit and watch. You didn't say anything about following."

"Don't worry." Peg eased into the line of cars leaving the lot. "She won't see us—and it won't take long. I'm pretty sure I know the type of place she's going and what she'll do there. I just want to make sure I'm right."

"Right about what?"

"Trust me."

There was silence, and Peg took her eyes off the Dodge way up ahead to glance at David's profile. "Think you can do that?"

He stroked the line of her chin. "I'm working on it."

She wanted to give him a smile, but she didn't dare look away again. You could lose someone in a blink.

After a few more miles, when the roads got darker and quieter, Peg let the van turn without following it. Feeling David's curious eyes on her, she threaded her way to a spot she calculated was one street over from Hewitt's destination. She felt a

135

thrill of satisfaction when she made her final turn and saw the van a block away, just dousing its lights.

"Bingo," David said softly, admiringly. "Where the hell are we?"

"These are rented garages. I know a few places around the city where they have them, and I was banking on this bunch because they're closest to the store. Now, unless I'm way off, she'll pull her Ford out of that garage and put the van in."

They watched from Peg's darkened car while Shirley Hewitt did exactly that.

"Unbelievable," David said with awe.

"I don't think she's through yet. She's going to get into the van and come out in another outfit."

David looked at her, then back at the garage. In five minutes Hewitt came out in a dress coat and high heels, carrying her shoulder bag. She closed the garage and drove off in the Ford.

David asked, "How in hell's name did you know she'd change?"

"Logic. She can't come home from work every night to a building like yours in dirty jeans. The other tenants, not to mention Hassan, would ask questions. And I'll bet you something else," Peg said, starting the car. "I'll bet that every week or so her shoulder bag goes home with a little extra in it."

"But the guard searched the bag. We saw him."

"I didn't say she took anything out of the *store* in her bag. I said she took it *home*. If Shirley Hewitt isn't boosting dresses in her vacuum cleaner, I'm Phil Donahue."

CHAPTER EIGHT

"But why not?" Peg asked.

David poured her more anisette. "I keep telling you why not. I'm a firm believer in following—"

"Established procedure," she finished for him. "And I respect that, really I do. But—"

"You don't look like you respect it," he said with a grin. "You look as if it's something you try when your first eight choices don't work."

"Well, I admit I'm not as conservative as you are."

"Boy George is conservative compared to you, Peg."

"David—"

"Sorry," he said, "I was teasing. I have a lot of respect for the way you work; you impressed the hell out of me tonight when you had that woman psyched out right down the line. But the orthodox thing to do now would be to take your suspicions to your boss, wouldn't it?"

"But—"

"Wouldn't it?" he persisted.

"Yes," Peg said impatiently, "but only if I had an orthodox boss. You've seen Hugh Burgholtz in action—I could reason better with a rattlesnake. And you saw for yourself that what I have on Shirley Hewitt is a lot more than suspicion. It isn't that big a leap to getting some real evidence—and *that* Mr. Burgholtz can't argue with." She leaned back against David's couch and folded her arms.

"No," he said.

"Oh, David. You really won't help me?"

"I am helping you. I'm—"

"I know." She rolled her eyes. "You're saving me from myself, or some variation on that song. My mother always used to do that."

David picked up her glass and the anisette bottle. "Judging from the fixes you get into now, keeping you out of trouble as a kid must have been a full-time job for several people."

"No more anisette," she said. "I have to be at work early tomorrow, remember?" She yawned and got up wearily. "So that's your final word? You won't help me get evidence on Hewitt?"

"Of course it's my final word." He put his arm around her. "Do I sound tentative?"

"No." She laughed. "You never do. But look, what if I came up with a plan that was really simple? Some safe little way to—"

"Let's get serious," David said. "We're not playing Clue here; we're talking about a criminal, aren't we? That rules out safe little anything."

"I mean relatively safe. Safer than a confrontation. Less safe than, oh, going to the zoo."

"You're still not being serious, Peg. That in itself bothers me. I don't want anything to happen to you; I want you to be on guard."

"I've told you," she said, raising her voice to reach

him as he brought their glasses into the kitchen. "I'm more careful than you think."

"Maybe." He came back out. "But the *most* careful way to handle this would be to go to your boss. Convince him you're right. Let *him* decide how to get the evidence."

She sighed and picked up the hated coat. David took it and helped her into it. The thing sure felt good; if only no one had to look at her.

"Will you do that?" he asked.

"I'll see," she grumbled.

"Good." He nuzzled her ear. "When can I see you again?"

"Mmm. In ten minutes?"

He chuckled. The rich sound vibrated against her throat. "I'm willing."

"No, you're not. You have to get up for work too."

"I don't care."

"Yes, you do."

"The hell I do. I may be a conservative man, but I'm still a man. Just say the word—I'll make love to you all night and be glad all day tomorrow."

Peg looked at him. "You really mean that, don't you?"

He looked back, his eyes hot. "Try me."

She didn't answer, and he put his hands inside her coat and lifted the ski sweater she still wore. She felt the warm press of his fingers on her back. Then they moved up and he gripped her bare shoulders and brought her close. His mouth opened and covered hers, and his tongue entered to softly probe and possess.

When he finally let her go, she knew that if she didn't back away this minute, she'd never leave. Already the swelling heat she could feel through her clothes and his was making her weak with wanting.

Just one more kiss, her heart said, but her mouth said, "I have to go. Now."

"All right, love," he said with a lazy smile. "I won't stop you."

"I might stop me," she mumbled to herself.

"What?"

"Never mind."

"How about Saturday night?" he said. "We'll have a swim. You've never seen the pool upstairs."

"What's it like?"

He began buttoning her coat. Peg wished it were some more intimate piece of clothing, and that he were unbuttoning it. "It's on the roof, in a glass bubble. The lights are kept low at night, except for the tanning lamps, so you can enjoy the view of the city while you swim."

"It sounds wonderful. I'd love to."

"Good. I'll make you dinner first."

"Um, no, thanks," she said, remembering the charred steak mittens and water-logged salad. "I have to work late."

"I'll wait," he said agreeably.

"No, I— You'd better not. I'll just eat in the staff cafeteria."

"Don't be silly," he said, opening the door for her. "I don't mind waiting. Unless you'll get too hungry yourself, working such a long day."

"Yes, that's it," she said. "I need to keep my energy up."

140

"I can understand that." They went out into the hall and he rang for the elevator. He took her in his arms and pushed her hair back to kiss her neck. "Especially since I have plans for your energy."

"What do you want, Bailey?" Hugh Burgholtz snapped. "I'm busy."

Peg closed the security office door. "I'd like to talk to you when you have a—"

"Are you deaf?" He leaned toward her from behind his desk like a belligerent bullfrog. His scalp showed through his few strands of hair in gleaming patches. "I said I'm busy."

"I heard you. But you didn't hear me. I said I'd like to see you when it's—"

"For God's sake, Bailey. How many times do I have to say it? I'm occupied. In conference. Out to lunch. Don't slam the door on your way out."

"You again?"

"*Yes*," Peg said. "I was last here at eleven this morning. It's four thirty now. Can I talk to you? Or can we at least set a time—"

"Catch me next week," he said, waving her off as if she were a housefly.

"Mr. Burgholtz," she said firmly, clasping her hands together to prevent one of them from picking up an ashtray and heaving it at him, "I have to talk to you about an important security matter."

Something in her voice must have penetrated. He lifted his head and looked at her. "What important security matter?"

Peg took a deep breath. "It's about the gowns. I have a very good idea who—"

The phone on Burgholtz's desk buzzed and he grabbed it. "Security. Yeah. Yeah. Where? Yeah."

He slammed it down. "Gotta go," he said, grabbing his suit jacket and attacking the sleeves with his stubby arms.

Peg said, "But when can—"

"Saturday," he said, pulling open the door.

"What time?" she called, but he was gone.

"Yeah, Bailey? What is it?"

Peg determinedly sat down on the only chair in the office that wasn't covered with papers and/or dirt. "I have a security matter to discuss. You told me to come in today."

"Uh-huh," Burgholtz said, looking around the room as if searching for an escape hatch. "Do it fast, will you?"

"Of course." She'd rehearsed and streamlined her statement to make her point briefly and persuasively. She was going to convince the security chief to set up focused surveillance of Shirley Hewitt. "I believe I know who's boosting the gowns. It's one of the—"

The radio crackled, and he picked it up. "Burgholtz."

"This is John Nicholas. I'm in Lamps and Mirrors. They need you at the order desk."

"On the way," he said, putting the radio in his pocket.

"Could you give me one more minute?" Peg

asked, her voice shaking with frustration. "This is important!"

He paused at the door. "What's it about, again? You know who's grabbing the gowns?"

"I think I do. I—"

"Well, which is it, Bailey? Do you know or don't you?"

"I'm reasonably sure," she said with dignity.

Burgholtz snorted. " 'Reasonably' and fifty cents will get you two phone calls. Come back when you have something to tell me." He hurried off.

"Bad day?" David asked as soon as he opened the door.

Peg tried to smile. The muscles didn't seem to be working. "I guess it shows."

"About the same as if you'd suddenly grown another ear. Sit down. Wine?"

"Please," she said gratefully. She hadn't had any dinner—she'd forgotten she'd planned to go to the cafeteria until it was time to leave—but she didn't dare tell David. Maybe he'd serve a snack with the wine—something straight from a box.

He came out of the kitchen with a bottle and two big goblets. "We don't have to swim if you don't feel like it," he said, twisting the corkscrew.

"But I do. I've been looking forward to it."

"Terrific," he said. His smile made her heart jump in spite of her mood. "So have I. Well, what went wrong today?"

"Mr. Burgholtz," she said, pronouncing the name as though it were a disease. "I went to see him about Shirley Hewitt."

"You did?" David asked, pleased. "So you took my advice. I'm glad. How did it go?"

She took a big swallow of wine. "How do I look?"

"Oh. So that's what's got you. What did he do?"

"Nothing much. He merely greeted me as if I were selling encyclopedias, refused to listen to a word, acted like a disgusting rude pig, and practically threw me out of his office. Other than that," she said, lifting her glass, "everything went fine."

"What a moron."

"I'm so frustrated. I know what the woman is up to—she did exactly what I thought she would if she was guilty. The store is losing at least one gown a week that costs a thousand dollars or two or three. And she has to be a pro to pull this off; she's not some poor misguided thing committing her first crime. But I can't *move.*"

She punctuated her words with a thump on the coffee table that rattled her empty glass. David steadied it and poured some more.

"There must be something," he said. He went to the kitchen and came back with a dish of pretzel sticks. "We'll put our heads together."

"Let's try just yours first. Mine is sore from banging against the wall." She eyed the pretzels hungrily but made herself wait a ladylike few seconds before taking some.

"How about talking directly to the police? Can you do that?"

She grimaced. "I'd be fired for certain. Mr. Burgholtz always tells us, 'The only time you go over my head is to pray.'"

"What about other Smith-Clove detectives? If you

tell them, somebody should be able to catch her in the act."

Peg started to answer, but a large bite of pretzels made that impossible. A speck flew out of her mouth and landed on the couch. Fortunately David had turned to get the wine bottle; she brushed it off before he saw.

She tried again to answer, but all that came out was, "Mither Boogo . . ."

"What?" David asked, turning back.

This time she made sure to swallow. "Mr. Burgholtz would consider it going over his head if I made some sort of formal case. But I can't just pass the word, either, because then I lose control over who knows. Also, on the small chance I'm wrong—well, you get the idea."

She took more pretzels and another sip of wine. "I did ask my detective friend to keep her eyes peeled, but she wasn't up for helping me out with any plan. Burgholtz has everybody so intimidated, they won't hiccup without his okay."

David brought the empty pretzel dish to the kitchen and refilled it. Peg tried to remember whether he'd eaten any himself. She didn't think so.

"You seem to like these," he said. "Are you hungry? I have pork chops left from dinner."

"No, thanks. I just happen to love pretzels." She didn't, but she was so famished she would have devoured anything, as long as it wasn't from David's stove. Thirsty, too; the salt, probably. She drained her glass.

"Well, Peg, I hate to sound like a broken record, but you should consider your friend's point of view.

145

Going through channels is a solid system—all businesses run on it. I think she's sensible to follow the rules."

Peg sighed. It was a good thing the wine had relaxed her or she'd be awfully tense. She was so tired of hearing how important it was to do her job by the book. First David, then Mr. Burgholtz, then Darcy, then David again.

"Look, why don't you give it one more shot?" he said. He refilled her glass, then reached over and took her hand. "I'll bet you can make the jerk listen if you state your case right. Take my word for it—I sell properties by knowing how to approach people. You have to decide precisely what you want to say, then condense it into a persuasive—"

"I tried that."

"Try again," David said. "You didn't show him you meant business. Use a firm—"

"I *did*. I tried *three times* to talk to him. I rehearsed and condensed until I was talking to my shoelaces. Will you trust me, for heaven's sake?"

He looked at her. "I do trust you."

"I don't mean in general," Peg said, pushing her hair back. "I wish you'd trust me not to just—blunder around and behave impulsively. Please take what I'm saying at face value. I'm reliable. I do plan things and research what I need. I've done my absolute best to deal with Mr. Burgholtz, and it—"

"Let's go," David said. He took her empty glass from her hand. He pulled her up from the couch and kissed her cheek.

"Where?" Everything in the room teetered for a

minute, and she held David's hand tight until the feeling passed.

"To the pool. We'll change and have a swim—it's just what we need."

Suddenly a plunge into cool depths *was* just what she needed. She could almost feel the water now, stroking her skin, soothing away the heaviness behind her eyes.

She'd remembered to take a suit this morning, her favorite black one that dipped low in back. She went into the bathroom and put it on, slipping her blouse over it. When she came out, David was in his maroon suit and nothing else. She had to lean against the door frame for support, and not just because the room was rocking again. His naked chest and legs, his strong back, the incredible appeal of his wide-shouldered form made her weak. All of it pushed her back to the wonder of her first sight of him in the store.

David smiled and took her in his arms. He eased her blouse off her shoulder and bit it, then moved along to her neck in a trail of kisses.

"David," she said, pressing closer.

"I love you, Peg," he whispered.

His hands were touching her with fire. She shifted to offer him her mouth and he took it, then brushed his lips over hers, back and forth.

"This is a taste. A promise," he said quietly. "A promise for later."

"Mmm," Peg said. Part of her wanted to make love with David this minute, but that swim sounded so good. And afterward, refreshed and relaxed, they'd come back down here, to his bedroom. . . .

*　*　*

They took the elevator to the twenty-fifth floor. Peg could smell chlorine and moist warmth. David pulled open a door, and suddenly they were in another world.

The pool was enclosed in a giant transparent dome. Lush plants hung at all levels, trailing sherbet-color tropical flowers. Between the weave of greenery and hot color, the night sky with its lights showed through the dome.

A few people swam and floated in the long free-form body of azure water; others sat under tanning lamps on lounge furniture that matched the floral rainbow overhead. Except for the lamps and what starlight penetrated, the dome was dark. Peg felt as if she'd stepped into a jungle night.

"It's incredible," she said. "So romantic and—just incredible!"

David smiled. "Let's swim."

She dived in. The water was delicious, warmer than she'd expected but with a shiver of coolness. When she surfaced, David was there. He took off down the length of the pool in a confident crawl, and she followed.

She couldn't match him for speed and didn't try; she wanted most to clear her increasingly woolly head. Gradually she found her arms and legs moving in a slow rhythm. It was nice; she could do this all night, just fishtail along in fluid luxury, pampered by the heat of the lamps and the perfume of gardenias.

She found her tempo changing, speeding up, and she realized why: someone had a radio on, and the slow song she'd been swimming to had become a rock number. She ought to slow down; she didn't want to get out of breath.

Peg looked to see what David was doing. He was thirty or forty feet away, just swimming at his own pace, paying no attention to the music.

If he could do that, so could she. She treaded water for a minute to break her rhythm and start over, then took off again, concentrating on regaining the comfortable pace of the earlier song.

But she soon found that whatever inner metronome David heard, she didn't have one—the rock beat was irresistible. She grew tired and climbed out.

Dripping, she started along the pool edge toward the chaise longue where she and David had left their things. As she approached, she saw that the person with the radio was sitting just beyond her chair. A new song came on, another good rocker, and she moved to the music as she walked, snapping her fingers.

The man with the radio was seventyish and gray-haired. Peg was surprised to see someone that age listening to hard rock, but when she reached him she realized he wasn't listening; he was asleep on his lounger.

She'd meant to get her towel and dry off, but the pounding drum was so enticing, she couldn't stop moving. It was good and loud up close, too.

Her body wanted to dance and she let it, her feet going faster, her arms shimmying. She felt numerous sensations at once—the pebbled cement under her feet, the scented pool air swirling past her, the droplets of water on her face and limbs, her wet suit caressing her skin. She was exhilarated; her head wasn't fuzzy now. She felt she could dance any step, no matter how complex.

A nearby plant trailed blossoms within reach. They were big and full, feathered fans of red. Without interrupting her rhythm, she picked one and reached around to put the stem inside her suit, right where it dipped over her bottom.

She danced on, her arms, legs, and hips gyrating with a beat of their own. They were the rulers; she just went along. Some people walked by, and she thought of inviting them to dance, too, but by the time she'd opened her mouth to ask, they were going out the exit door. Another person passed and then another, but they seemed to be in a hurry.

She caught sight of David at the far end of the pool, starting back her way. She thought he was swimming faster than he had been but it was probably her imagination. Everything seemed fast now; the music was a rhythm machine, making her jump and dip and spin.

Her wet hair slapped her cheeks as she twirled. Some drops flew at the gray-haired man, and suddenly he opened his eyes, took one look at the sopping wet woman with the red blossom peeking from the back of her suit gyrating just inches from him, jumped up, grabbed his radio, and stumbled off toward the exit.

"Peg!" she heard. She turned and saw David behind her in the water, lost her balance, and fell in.

When she came up, everything looked different. The water felt lovely, but the furniture, the plants, and even David were all leaning at the same strange angle. Holding the edge, she tilted her head right and then left, trying to get into the picture, but that only made the angle worse. Her head felt as if someone had packed it with leaves.

"You're looped," David said.

She nodded. It hurt, so she let go of the edge to hold her head, and promptly sank. Then she felt David's strong grip under her arms. He lifted her to the surface and placed her hands on the edge.

"Don't let go," he said.

She nodded again, and winced. "Everything's tipping," she said.

"I don't doubt it. You knocked back an awful lot of wine."

He was right. And what he didn't know was that she'd knocked it back on an empty stomach.

She fixed foggy eyes on David. "Are you mad at me?"

"Well, hell," he said, "I live here, Peg. I have to face these people who just watched my tipsy girlfriend boogie around the pool with a flower in her tush."

She closed her eyes. The lids felt like pottery. "Was that why people left?"

"You bet. You cleared the place."

Peg glanced around. He was right; there wasn't a soul. "I'm so sorry," she said. "I can't believe I embarrassed you again."

He looked away. Peg felt awful. She tried to think of something else to say, to get across how much she cared for him and wanted to be dignified for him,

151

but her brain didn't seem to be working any better than anything else was.

Then she heard an unexpected sound. She realized David was laughing.

"I keep thinking of that guy's face," he said. "The guy with the radio. What does a man that age think when he wakes up out of a sound sleep to find a nearly naked woman spraying water on him?" He laughed harder, throwing his head back.

After a startled moment Peg began to laugh, too, quietly at first, and then louder. David put his arms around her, and she gratefully let go of the pool edge and rested her hands on his big shoulders, still shaking with giggles.

Soon she became aware that David's hands weren't just keeping her afloat. They were moving over her, pressing her to him. She snuggled her head on his neck.

"I love you so much," he said.

"I love you too. And I'm sorry—I promised myself I wouldn't do anything like that to you again."

"I'm getting better at dealing with it," he said.

"You know," she said, "I think you are. Ouch—my head."

Gently he rubbed it where it rested on his shoulder. "Is everything still tipping?"

"Yes. What was I saying?"

"That I'm getting better."

"Definitely. You don't embarrass as easily anymore."

"I'll show you how easily I don't embarrass now," he said. "Come on."

"Where?" she asked, her eyes half closed.

"Just float. I'll pull you."

He brought her down the pool to where she could just stand. He kissed her, his tongue doing wonderful things, sweetly tangling with hers. Then she felt his hands on her buttocks. She whispered, "What . . . ?"

"Shh," he said. "Hold on to the edge and lift your knees up."

"But—"

"Just do it."

She did as he instructed, and a moment later her suit was still on in front but he'd slipped the bottom off.

Peg was still muddled, but not so much that she didn't know she'd suddenly been rendered half naked in a public pool. "David!" she said. "What do you think you're—"

Before she could finish, she found out exactly what. In a flash he'd removed his own suit. She felt his bare body against her, the water swirling between them.

"There," he said. He reached under her suit and caressed her breasts, swishing the water over them. "Doesn't that feel good? This is in the way. Might as well take the whole thing off." He pulled the suit over her head and dropped it.

Peg watched it sink. "We're both naked," she said wonderingly.

He laughed. "You sure think slowly with half a bottle of wine under your belt. Excuse me, under your pretty navel." He touched it, and she trembled.

She asked, "Are we, um, going to . . ."

"You bet." He took her earlobe into his mouth and wrapped his arms around her.

"Here?"

"Mm-hm."

"What if someone comes in?"

"Nobody will. You chased them all out."

"You're not serious. We aren't really—"

"Yes. We are. Now, be quiet." He took her hands and pulled them up behind his neck, dropping his own hands to her hips and running them teasingly along her sides on the way down. He stroked the place where she curved there, where her waist rounded out so attractively. Then he held her bottom and pressed himself hard against her.

"David," she breathed.

He didn't speak. He covered her mouth with his, gently forcing hers wide open. He held her head while he kissed her, twining his fingers in her wet hair. She felt his tongue as it explored, and then boldly did some exploring of her own. Between the wine and the water and the soft dimness and the intoxicating tropical fragrance, she was beyond restraint.

She touched his back, thrilling to the tough cords of muscle, the way his flesh flared to the athletic swell of his buttocks. Once again she flashed back to that day at the store, his tantalizing nude body just inches from her eyes, and as warmth coursed through her, she held him tighter.

She heard a noise and quickly turned. Someone was opening the pool door.

"David!" she said.

He looked up and she nodded toward the door.

They watched as the man she'd awakened came in and hurried over to his chair.

She tried to pull away, but David held on to her. "He's fifty feet away," he whispered.

Peg felt a flush heat her cheeks in spite of the cool water. "But David, good grief, we're—"

"No, we aren't. Not yet. As soon as he leaves."

The flush deepened. "I didn't mean that. I mean we're nude."

"He doesn't know. Look, he's just getting his shoes. He's handling this fine. See how you toughened him up? Now he's going to the door. He's opening it. At last. Now . . . now, love. . . ."

She gasped as he shifted her body with eager hands and made them one. He groaned against her mouth.

Surely she was going to drown—drown in the miracle that was David, David and herself and what they were together. She wrapped her arms tighter around his neck and arched to meet his thrusts. She was caught in a whirlpool of delight, spiraling away to a place she'd never been, but secure with David for her guide.

He was saying her name over and over, and his breathing was quickening in her ear. As they moved faster, the water moved, too, echoing their ecstatic rhythm.

Then Peg could feel all of David—against her, around her, within her. His voice was harsh with the strength of his feeling, and she knew she was speaking, too, but the words formed themselves in the language of passion. A second later she cried out in the jungle darkness, and David's cry followed.

The water calmed as the lovers did, and on the widening ripples that faded across the pool, a red blossom floated.

CHAPTER NINE

David was waiting where they'd arranged, a block over from Ashford Avenue. Peg parked behind him and got into the Lincoln.

"I hope you're right that tonight's the night," he said.

"It has to be. I've studied those cleaning assignment sheets for hours, and every single time a gown has disappeared, Shirley Hewitt was in the group assigned to that end of the floor. I *know* she'll take one tonight."

"I don't like it. I don't like anything about this. And I don't see how you can be so sure."

Peg buckled her seat belt. "I promise you, in less than an hour she'll pull into that garage of hers with what she thinks is a lot more than dirt in her vacuum cleaner. But the vacuum won't be there, because we'll have taken it out of the van with us at one of these stoplights along here. And then I'll have my proof." She touched David's hand on the wheel. "Thank you for helping me get it."

"Don't thank me yet," he said. "This is far from over. Any one of a thousand things could go wrong."

"Nothing will. And even if it did," she said, moving over to snuggle against him, "I'm thanking you for what you already did. For agreeing to help."

David laughed without humor. "'Agreeing to help' isn't quite accurate. You know damn well I had no choice."

"But—"

"I didn't, Peg. Not if I wanted you to be safe—or as safe as possible. If there were any way in hell I could have prevented you from doing this, I would have."

And did he ever try, Peg thought. She remembered the arguments, night after night of David working on her with his implacable logic. She'd fought back just as implacably, fixated on her determination to expose Hewitt and stop the thievery.

She'd never managed to bring David over to her side, but she *had* convinced him that she was going to carry out her plan with him or without him. That had been enough; he simply wouldn't let her do it alone.

David turned off Ashford Avenue. They'd be at Smith-Clove in five minutes. Peg's pulse began to speed up; she was exhilarated and eager to get going. Tonight, finally, she'd have evidence on Hewitt; Mr. Burgholtz would have to accept it, and she'd make sure to claim her rightful credit. Most important, she'd feel the deep satisfaction of having done outstanding work despite the obstacles and of saving Smith-Clove thousands of dollars in further thefts.

"You're *really* sure about the timing?" David asked.

"Yes," Peg said patiently. "Those assignment sheets are like a map. This is the first time Hewitt's been sent to that area in nine days. She'll take a gown."

"I don't know," he said, shaking his head. "This whole show has disaster written all over it."

"Oh, come on. Even you can't argue with that reasoning."

"The reasoning isn't the point," he said, slowing for a woman crossing the street. They were about three blocks from the store. "If it were me, I wouldn't dare grab the thing now. She must know the heat's on. Even an idiot can see the extra security activity, right? I'd back off until things settled down."

"That's because you're a sensible person and not a thief," Peg said. She drummed her fingers on the door handle while they waited for a bus in front of them to move. "The criminal brain doesn't work that way. She'll want to hustle while she still can. Don't forget, nobody suspects her but me, and she doesn't know I do. Besides, it's an ego thing—sometimes having security breathing down their necks adds to the challenge. A lot of thieves feel invincible."

"You think Hewitt does?"

Peg shrugged. "It fits. She's a pro, she's bold and daring. This isn't some mouse snitching rubber bands when the boss is at lunch."

They turned into the staff lot. David parked well away from Hewitt's van and they got out. Moving quickly, as Peg had prepared him to do, he followed her along the fence to the van. With a thin awl, the way she'd practiced doing on her neighbor's van, she got the back door lock open, and they climbed in.

Peg used her penlight flash just long enough for a sweep of the inside. It looked just as it had the night they'd watched Hewitt leave work, crowded with heavy-duty equipment convenient to hide behind. There were industrial floor polishers, mops, and brooms. Half a dozen upright vacuums were stacked near the front, and a portable metal closet stood in a back corner.

Peg opened it and flashed the light. It was crammed with cleaning products—no room for the two of them. She closed the door and gave the thing a push; it moved easily. That was it, then—they'd hide behind the closet. Hewitt would never spot them when she put her things inside.

"What now?" David asked.

"Help me move this so we can go around it. Then we just sit tight."

Together they eased the closet forward. They got behind it.

"Great," Peg said. "Plenty of room."

"Your coat," David said, brushing at it. She looked down. Enough light came in through the high windows so she could see the smudge of dirt on the greenish yellow wool. "How come you wore this?" he asked. "You could ruin it." He himself was dressed perfectly for the occasion, in jeans and a heavy leather jacket.

"It's all I have," she said, picturing her old coat, the one that had almost been incinerated, hanging forlornly in her closet.

"What about your jacket?"

"My jacket?"

"The one you wore when we went skiing. It was navy blue, with a snowflake pattern."

She knew what he meant; she was stalling for time because she didn't want him to know how inefficient she'd been in this aspect of her plan for the evening. Her ski jacket would have been much better for tonight than her long, bright coat, but it was at the cleaners!

"Oh, that one," she said finally. "I, um, lent it to Diane. She's going skiing."

"Where? There's no snow. It rained all last week."

"Not around here. She went to—to Aspen."

"Aspen? Diane? The one who hangs towels over her windows because she can't afford curtains?"

Peg was sorry she'd started this. Groping for a new topic, she said, "Did I tell you about my fail-safe idea?"

"No," David said. "What do you mean?"

She shifted her shoulder out of the corner it was wedged into. "My backup in case of a problem. I wrote—"

"'In case of a problem'?" he repeated suspiciously.

"There won't be one. I told you that. Relax. But you just don't ever move without covering yourself in this kind of work."

"I won't relax and you shouldn't either. Would you relax with sharks circling your boat?" His tone was short, but Peg sensed that he was reassured by the idea of an established structure for the work, even if the business was a far cry from real estate.

"I wrote Darcy a note—Darcy Carter, my friend in security," she said. "I told her about Hewitt and explained my plan—how I'd be in the van with an associate, and we'd take the vacuum and gown out when she stopped for one of the lights on Ashford, and my car would be parked nearby."

"Why a note? Why not just tell her?"

"I did that on purpose," Peg said with pride. "Darcy is kind of a company person, and she won't cross the boss. He scares her. That time you helped me follow Hewitt, I tried to get Darcy; she wasn't home, but she probably wouldn't have come, since it wasn't an actual assignment. So I never told her what direction I was following on the thefts, since it was unofficial. Could you move your arm down? A little more."

"How's this?"

"Fine. It won't be much longer, anyway—once Hewitt puts her stuff in here, we can move. So, back to Darcy. I stuck the note in her locker. Her shift ends about now, when it's too late to try to talk me out of this. I owed her that; she'd be so worried, she'd feel obligated to stop me."

She heard a sound and stopped talking to listen. Yes, there it was—a buzz of voices.

"The cleaning people are getting out," she whispered. "Hear them? Let's stay really quiet now."

They waited behind the closet, the smells of disinfectant and polish surrounding them. Soon there was a metallic rattle at the double doors. Peg held her breath; David seemed to stop breathing too.

The doors opened. Peg sneaked a look from her dark corner and saw Shirley Hewitt silhouetted in the light, lifting her supplies in. The doors closed, and Hewitt got into the cab. The engine started and they moved off.

Peg exhaled in a *whoosh*. "Let's get started," she said quietly, slipping out. "We have five minutes to confirm that the gown is in the vacuum. Then, as soon as she stops for a light on Ashford, we get out with both things and go to my car. And congratulate ourselves."

"Don't be smug. It might not be so easy to congratulate ourselves with knives in our throats. You're sure she won't hear us getting out?"

"No, not with all the traffic noise. But even if she does, it won't matter—I'll have the proof. My two-way radio is in my car, and the first thing I'll do is raise Mr. Burgholtz. As long as the gown is in my hands, he'll bring the police right in. Okay, let's see how that vacuum opens."

"Which one?"

Peg followed David's eyes. He was looking at the stack of vacuums.

Her pulse skipped. There was no way to tell which of them Hewitt had used tonight.

She forced down her panic and made herself think. If they had to open each one, they'd never finish in time. Of course, they could take the whole bunch, but that would be idiotic.

There was nothing to do but start, and hope. They each took a machine and tried to open the part that held the bag—and, Peg prayed, something besides the bag. Every one seemed to latch differently, and they worked awkwardly in the uneven gray light. A cloud of grit slowly filled the van; Peg felt it in her mouth and eyes.

"How much more time?" David asked.

She peered at her watch. "Two minutes."

The van stopped.

"Ashford?" he asked. "Already?"

Peg shook her head. "Can't be."

"But there shouldn't be a stop before then."

"A car must have pulled out in front of us or something," she said. "Wait—did you hear that? A door closed. Probably a car on the street with an open door, and Hewitt couldn't pass in a thing this big."

As if to confirm her guess, the van started moving.

"Back to work," Peg said, opening another vacuum. She pulled the front away—and felt something soft. Hardly daring to breathe, she grabbed her penlight.

"David, look!" she whispered.

He leaned over. Shiny kelly green fabric, protected by plastic wrap, was nestled beside the vacuum bag.

"Nice going," he said with grudging admiration.

Excitement flooded her. Now that it had really happened—now that she'd been proved right—she couldn't wait for this to be over. Her hands shook as she tried to close the machine. It wouldn't fit back together.

"Leave it this way," David said. "We can take the thing open if we have to. Give it to me and let's get ready to leave."

"I'd like to hold it," Peg said. Just then it snapped shut. She scrambled up, clutching the vacuum as if it were a priceless heirloom. She stood with David at the doors, her heart banging. Any second now the van would stop, and she'd have won. She had the evidence; the thefts were over.

They rode on, the van bumping along the avenue. Now Peg was sure Hewitt wouldn't hear them get out, with all the racket the equipment made.

"What if she doesn't come to a red light?" David asked.

Peg said, "Have you ever driven up Ashford without hitting one?"

"No," he said.

Passing street lamps gave just enough light so she could see his face. It was dirty. She was filthy herself; she could feel it. She ached to get home and take her clothes off and shower.

Something was tugging at her mind. She was so intent on preparing to jump when the van stopped that she didn't pay attention. But as they rode on and her unease grew, it came to her: she was afraid David was right. They'd gone much too far without stopping. As incredible as it was, maybe they'd come all the way up Ashford Avenue on a whole string of greens.

But was that possible? Weren't the lights computer-timed for traffic flow?

Or it might be her perspective that was off. Did the van only *seem* to have traveled so far? Judging distance was hard when you couldn't see the road.

"I'm going to peek out," she told David. He frowned but didn't say anything. She laid the vacuum gently on the floor and started toward a window. The van lurched, and she grabbed the closet to steady herself. Her perspective *was* haywire; she not only couldn't gauge distance but speed either. They seemed to be going much faster than the thirty or thirty-five miles an hour people traveled on busy Ashford.

She stood on tiptoe to look out. The glass was filthy and it was hard to see what they were passing. She watched telephone poles fly past and tried to get her bearings.

She knew Ashford Avenue almost as well as she knew her kitchen, but from this angle she was stymied. Nothing looked familiar. She kept watching, standing as tall as she could. Any minute she'd spot a landmark. They should be somewhere around the water company building . . . or maybe as far as Teller Park. She looked to the side to see if there were trees in the distance and got a lash in her eye. She rubbed it away and looked again.

A cold knot was forming in her stomach. She felt it before she knew why it was there, but the reason surfaced a moment later.

They weren't on Ashford Avenue. She couldn't tell where they were.

"David," she said.

"Yes?"

"Something's wrong."

He spun to face her. "What's the matter?"

"We're not on Ashford. I don't know what street this is, but it's getting more deserted every minute. She must know we're in here."

He walked back to her, holding on to things for

166

support. "Aren't you jumping to a conclusion? So she took a different route. Why does that mean she knows?"

"It isn't just a different route," Peg said miserably. "She's driving fast. Not speeding—she wouldn't risk a ticket—but I think she's purposely using streets where she won't have to stop, and going fast enough so we don't dare jump out."

"Hell," David said.

She had to admire him; he seemed annoyed but not afraid. For herself, the implications of what she'd just put together were sickening. She felt sweat mixing with the dirt on her face.

He said, "Let's move back to the doors. There's still a chance you're wrong. I don't want to be caught off guard if we do stop."

They made their way back, and Peg picked up the vacuum. They stood and waited. She wanted to touch David, to have the comforting warmth of a quick hug or even the brush of his hand, but she resisted; he probably didn't feel much warmth for her right now.

The van bounced, and Peg moved her feet apart for balance. Was it her imagination, or had they picked up still more speed? She glanced at the window. The shadows did seem to be flickering faster.

"How could she know?" David asked. "You made it sound as if she couldn't possibly find out."

"I know. But it's the only answer that fits what's happening."

He said, "We're slowing down."

She looked toward the window. He was right.

"Get ready," he said.

She stood, tight with tension, gripping the vacuum. The van rumbled to a halt. Before it stopped moving, Peg had the doors open. David jumped out and helped her down.

"Look," she whispered, "the garages! She *was* just taking a different route!"

He said, "Give me the vacuum and let's get out of—"

"*Hold it!*"

They spun around. A blond woman was crouched, feet apart, holding a revolver in both hands.

Peg cried, "Darcy!"

David said, "Ohh."

Peg said, "Where—How did—Oh, no, Darcy, not you."

"Shut up," Darcy said.

Shirley Hewitt came around the other side of the van.

"You stopped for her," Peg accused. "I thought I heard a door closing after we left the lot, and it was the van door, wasn't it? You picked up Darcy. But how did you know we were in there?"

"She didn't," Darcy said. "Nobody would have, but your helpful little note told me everything. I just didn't get it in time to stop Shirley from leaving. Of course," she went on angrily, turning to the other woman, "I wouldn't have had to flag you down or do any of this if you hadn't insisted on taking *one more stupid dress!* You moron!"

Shirley Hewitt shrugged. Her black curls tumbled over her shoulders. "It doesn't matter. The gown's not going anywhere." She reached for the vacuum. "Give me that."

"No!" Peg said, yanking it away.

"Yes, it *matters*," Darcy snapped. "Now we have to kill these two—and it's your fault."

Shirley rolled her eyes. "I'll kill them if it's too big a deal for you."

"Don't do anything. Wait till the guys get here."

Oh, no. Peg glanced at David and caught his eye. He seemed to follow her line of thought: if there were more people on the way, any move had to be made now. And after what they'd just heard, there was no choice. She didn't know how David could look so calm. Her stomach was quivering. She'd known for a while that they were in grave danger, but to actually hear the words "kill these two . . ."

Shirley grabbed for the vacuum again, and again Peg held it away. It was ridiculous to make a stand when she and David might be dead in minutes, but she wouldn't give the thing up. She'd worked too hard and long for it.

"Give it to me!" Shirley said.

"No! I don't have to."

"Yes, you do," a male voice said, and she and David turned to find two wide-shouldered men in jeans and parkas coming around the van.

"It's about time," Darcy said. "How long ago did I call you? Twenty minutes?"

"Relax," the shorter man said. He nodded toward Peg and David. "They're not in any hurry. They'll never be in a hurry again." He grinned, showing large discolored teeth.

Peg felt a chill on her back. Her knees threatened

to buckle. She took a deep breath and released it as slowly as she could, trying to let the sensation of control alleviate her tension.

But her brain must have been whirring even while the rest of her was rigid with fear, because she had an idea. She examined it, trying to decide the best way, calculate the timing, gauge the odds. She had to admit they weren't great.

But it was the only idea she had.

She didn't know if there were more than four in on the scam, and she didn't care to find out. It was worse facing four than one or two, but if the cast got bigger still, she and David wouldn't have a chance. It had to be now.

The taller man turned to Shirley. "You had to pull one more, huh? You couldn't wait for the next place. Now look where the hell we are."

"So *what?*" Shirley said. "All of you get the hell off my back."

Closer, Peg prayed, get closer together.

"First Darcy gives me a hard time, now you. *She* doesn't even have the guts to take the things."

Bunch up more. Just a little more.

"This baby is worth three thousand. Not bad for a last job." She reached for the vacuum in Peg's arms.

Her pulse pounding, Peg pulled the vacuum open. In almost the same motion she grabbed the bag and tore it, and a cloud of black dirt billowed out. She heard yelling and coughing as it hit everyone. Then she realized she was one of the people yelling. Her eyes burned terribly; she couldn't see.

She felt David's strong hand pulling her and she

170

ran, blindly following, still clutching the shell of the vacuum with the gown inside. He must have been the only one to shut his eyes in time. She was terrified; how far could she get without falling and breaking an ankle?

Then she was being lifted and David was climbing over her.

"Good," he said, "the keys." He started the van with a roar of the engine and sped off.

"Thank God," Peg said, brushing at her face. Her eyes stung terribly, but at least that made tears, and she was starting to get her vision back. "Look, I'm really sorry this happened, but—"

David stared straight ahead. "Don't talk. Don't say a word to me. I've had it with you."

She gasped. "No! Be reasonable, David! You're upset, of course you are—I am too. That was a terrifying experience. But at least—"

"There's no 'at least'!" he thundered, striking the dashboard with his hand. "Get it through your head —we almost got killed! Two lives could have been lost, just *gone*, and you're giving me 'at least'! Nothing matters next to that, do you hear me? Nothing!"

She was sniffing back tears, not only from the dirt. "But we didn't get killed, and we *won!* We have the vacuum and the gown, and I know enough for the police to find Shirley and Darcy, and maybe the men too. That isn't nothing!"

"You listen to me," David said, turning to shake his finger at her. The van swerved sharply, and he cursed and righted it with both hands. "You worked on me and worked on me until I agreed to help you with this crazy thing—and everything I warned you

171

about came true! Every one of your arguments was wrong! And because of that, *we're lucky to be alive!* Well, damn it, I'm going to let that be a lesson to me —I'll stay alive, and *alone!* I don't need some flake who has so little tolerance for sensible advice that she'll put her neck in a noose rather than take it!"

"David—"

"*Quiet!* Don't say another thing. That's *it!*"

Peg slid down in her seat and put her hands over her eyes as the tears came faster and faster.

CHAPTER TEN

"*Again?*" Ellen Bailey said. "Peg, what *has* gotten into you?"

"Mother, I just asked a question," Peg said, trying to contain her impatience. She was so edgy now.

"That wasn't 'just a question.' It would be 'just a question' if you asked, 'How's the weather down there?' or 'What are your plans for Easter?' or even 'How are you, Mom?'—which you didn't, I must point out. But—"

"I'm sorry," Peg said, rubbing her forehead. Her headache was worse. "I care how you are, you know I do."

"I do know, darling. I just can't resist laying on some guilt—it's a mother's privilege. But as I was saying, this is the second time in a couple of months you've called with what you must admit are uncharacteristic questions. How to clean a shirt, and now how to clean a coat. I was surprised the first time, but I restrained my curiosity—"

"No, you didn't. You didn't restrain anything."

"You're remembering wrong, dear. I was very discreet."

"Mother, you practically—oh, never mind. Can we just stick to what I asked?"

"The coat, you mean."

"Yes." Peg pulled her feet up under herself on the couch. Tentative fingers of April sunshine brightened the living room but only made her head hurt more. "Should I take it to a dry cleaner, or is it hopeless?"

"The coat is full of vacuum cleaner dirt?"

"Yes," she said. "Loaded with it. Greasy black guck."

"How did—wait, scratch that question. You'll never answer it. I guess the cleaners are worth a try."

"You think so?"

"Certainly. Why not?"

"The coat is really a mess, Mother. Shouldn't I just give up?"

"Well," her mother said, "I can't see the damage, of course, but I'd ask their opinion." She paused. "You know, dear, it almost sounds as if you don't *want* to get the coat clean. I know that's silly, but . . ."

"Oh," Peg said, trying for an offhand chuckle and producing only a strangled croak, "that is silly. But since you agree it's hopeless, I'll just get rid of the thing."

"But I didn't—"

"There's my doorbell," she said. "It must be Diane—she said she was coming over. I have to run."

They said their good-byes, and Peg went to let Diane in. She'd brought Blondie, and the dog seemed to remember the apartment, though she

174

hadn't been there since Peg had tried to train her with the mousetrap. Apparently it hadn't worked. Peg and Diane watched the exuberant dog leap from sofa to chair and back.

"I'm sorry," Diane said. "She's hard to train."

Peg hastily moved her teacup off the sofa end-table. "Did you try the mousetrap?"

"A few times. But I don't leave it for too long—I'm afraid someone will sit on it."

Peg coughed.

"Blondie, come here," Diane said. She took the dog onto her lap, trying to arrange its legs neatly. "Calm down. That's my girl. Show Peg how nicely you're growing up."

Peg looked at her ex-roommate. Her auburn hair was swept back to wave around her ears. She had on a royal blue knit dress and burgundy boots with slim heels.

"You look nice," she said, comparing Diane's style with her own slapped-together casualness. She wore no makeup, and her hair was clean but straight—she hadn't had the energy to coax it to curl.

"Thanks," Diane said. "You look—comfortable."

They stared at each other.

"Oh, hell," Diane said. "You look terrible."

Peg sighed. "I know."

"You're having trouble getting over this, aren't you?"

Peg didn't answer for a minute. She hadn't told Diane that David had left her; she couldn't bear to. The pain was so acute that to share it would be to relive it yet again.

"Oh, the robbery, you mean," she said.

"Of course. What else? Peg, I'm worried about you."

"Don't be. It was a scary experience, but it worked out well. I'll be fine. How about some tea?"

"I'd love some." Peg didn't move. "Would you like me to get it?"

"What? Oh. No, of course not." She went into the kitchen. Blondie jumped off Diane's lap and followed.

"Blondie, come back here," Diane called. "I'm sorry, Peg; she thinks the kitchen means food for her."

"I don't mind," she said. She put a tea bag in a cup and patted the dog's soft head.

"You will in a minute. She opens cabinets and chews things."

"You wouldn't do that," Peg said quietly. The dog gazed innocently up at her.

"I'll make her a bed to lie on," Diane said. "That'll keep her quiet. Can I take an old towel? Or how about this?"

"How about what?"

"This dirty blanket. Oh, it's a coat. Good grief, what happened to it?"

Peg brought in Diane's tea. "It got dirty."

"I can see that. Did a volcano erupt on it?"

Peg rubbed her forehead.

"Well, no problem," Diane said. "The cleaners will take care of it. I'll use a towel."

"No, use that. I'm throwing it out anyway."

"Throwing it out? This coat?"

"Yes," Peg said. She was going to deep-six the thing at last. Though the sight of it was painful, a

176

psychological tug had made her keep it these two weeks: to let go of it was to let go of David, for good.

She'd finally realized today that however much she subconsciously wished it were so, having control over the coat's fate didn't give her any over the relationship. The nonrelationship. It had been a tough decision to junk the coat, but it was made. Maybe she'd even have made it without manipulating her mother into helping.

"Can you at least try—"

"*No,*" Peg said.

"Well. All right. So," Diane said, brightening, "the congratulations must be pouring in. I'm so proud of you. You solved those thefts single-handed."

"Not quite." She drank some tea. It was cold. She remembered that she'd made it at least an hour ago.

"No thanks to your boss, though. How was he about it?"

Peg shrugged. "For him, very gracious—though Mr. Burgholtz is being gracious if he just doesn't pour coffee on you. I could tell he wanted to choke me, but what can he do when *his* bosses are sending me flowers?"

"They did that?"

Peg nodded. "Flowers and wine. I threw out the flowers yesterday, but they were beautiful while they lasted." The phrase stuck in her ears, reverberating; it was hard not to cry. "There was a whole case of wine—lovely French ones, red and white. I put it away for—for a special occasion."

Now she'd really cry if she didn't distract herself.

She went to the kitchen and put the flame on under the kettle.

"You must be a celebrity at the store," Diane said.

"Mm-hm." She looked down at Blondie, curled up against a cabinet on her towel. "Are you sad, too?" she asked the dog.

"What?" Diane said from the living room.

"Nothing." She poured her tea and sat on the couch again. The afternoon sun grew stronger, coloring the room, but she didn't notice. Diane tried to get her to go out for dinner—"My treat," she coaxed —but Peg wanted to be alone, and Diane finally left.

She thought about eating, checked herself for an appetite, and found none. She put on music. The rock beat she'd hoped would cheer her was jarring, and she changed the record to a soft one, but that depressed her more. Finally she turned off the stereo and sat in silence, watching the room get dark.

She'd worked harder the last couple of months than ever, but right now all she wanted was more work. She dreaded her second day off tomorrow. She had to find something to do; if she sat around again, she'd go batty. There had to be some good distracting activity that didn't require resources she didn't have right now, such as an attention span. Something that would fill the day and not make her think of David.

Because right now she hardly thought about anything else. He haunted her in day and night dreams. She supposed that would fade eventually, but how did a person function until "eventually" came?

She was still amazed that he blamed her for the

danger they'd landed in; only a compulsively over-cautious person would consider it her fault that she'd been betrayed by a trusted co-worker. She could have dealt with that, though, as she'd dealt all along with the chasm between his conservative, orderly ways and her offhand, impulsive personality. She'd thought he was dealing with it too.

But what she couldn't do anything about was the fact that he blamed her enough to leave her. She kept thinking back on the awful things he'd said in the van, the way he'd raved and shouted, his face dark with rage. He hadn't left the slightest room for doubt that he never wanted to hear her name again.

No matter how hatefully unfair that was, though, she'd stopped being angry. She had only one feeling left, and it was so powerful it blocked out all else. She missed him. She ached to have David back. She'd give anything to see him.

A spark flickered in the back of her mind. So she needed something to do tomorrow. What if she did it downtown, whatever it was? What if she did it around Valley Realty? What if she just happened to be finished doing it when David left the office at five?

She sat up. She'd be wearing her best, naturally—maybe the gray-and-silver sweater that went so well with the black pants. She'd do her makeup just right, really spend time on her hair so it would curl over her shoulders instead of hanging there like wet yarn.

She'd watch from up the block until he came out. She knew which way he walked to reach his car;

she'd start walking herself, and be "astonished" to run into him.

What would happen then? She swallowed, excitement building. The grayness was lifting.

He wouldn't be thrilled to see her at first, but he wouldn't ignore her; he'd stop and talk politely for a minute. If, in that minute, her presence brought enough memories to stir his feelings. . . .

She was getting hungry. She went to the kitchen and opened the refrigerator, but there wasn't much; she hadn't been to the market in so long, she'd forgotten when.

There was some pot roast in the freezer she'd made months ago. It looked fine—plenty of carrots and peas to put color in her cheeks. She put it into the microwave oven to defrost.

The oven hummed as she went to her room, got out the black pants, and laid them on the bed. They weren't wrinkled. She smoothed the velvety fabric.

The timer beeped and she walked back to the kitchen. She poked the meat, found it still partly frozen, and pushed the button again.

In her room she took out her gray sweater and put it with the pants. She held black boots and gray shoes next to the outfit. The boots were a better match, but the shoes were prettier, with open toes and high heels. Though if she had to hurry to bump into him, it might be smarter to . . .

Peg sank down on the bed, still holding the shoes and boots. She remembered the first time she'd ambushed David near his office. She'd fallen getting out of her car and made a spectacle of herself; then

180

she'd had to hurry to catch him, and her heels hadn't helped.

But mostly what she remembered was David's disgust when he discovered she'd engineered the meeting. He'd gotten around to feeling flattered eventually, but not before he'd used words like "infantile," "misguided," and "humiliating."

She got up and put the shoes and boots away, then the sweater and pants. What *had* she been thinking of? She wanted David back, so she was going to pull still another of the stunts that had driven him away every time?

Very good, Peg. If that's the best thinking you can do now, you're not safe on the street.

She went to the kitchen and put the untouched pot roast into the refrigerator. Then she leaned her head against the metal door and cried.

"Mr. Robertson, hello," Hassan said. "You sick or what? You never come home in lonchtime. I am putting car away?"

"No, thanks. I came for some papers I forgot this morning. I'll be leaving in a minute."

David went up, found the contracts he'd been going over the night before, and got back into the elevator. As the doors opened in the lobby, he realized he was still missing one. Ignoring Hassan's stare, he pushed the button for twenty.

Back in his apartment, he triple-checked to make sure he had everything before going back down. Damn it, that was the third time lately he'd misplaced important documents. His mind was mush.

He got into the Lincoln and headed back to the

office. He was sick of this; he had to get it together. He never used to be forgetful; nothing was the same anymore. His habits, his routine, the walls and corners of his life that he relied on to be there just weren't.

He didn't kid himself about the reason; he knew why as well as he knew his shoe size. It was Peg, and the way she'd disrupted his whole existence with her flakiness and immaturity. He'd tried to accept it, but in the end she'd made that impossible.

David had learned to overlook her embarrassing escapades. But embarrassment was one thing; danger was another. Her last little bit of poor planning and misjudgment had nearly gotten them killed. He'd finally seen the relationship realistically. He'd understood at last that it couldn't work.

Now he was getting her out of his system. It was harder than he'd expected—and he'd expected it to be a killer. Pictures came to him: he and Peg on the ski trail, her laughing face as she tried to learn . . . the mousetrap on her couch . . . and the pool, Peg dancing with abandon, a red flower at her bum . . . and then later . . . everything.

Well, so it would take even more time to forget her. He had plenty of that—and not much else to do with it.

There were times when he wondered if he ought to be thinking in another direction. Lying sleepless late at night, or finding some sharp reminder of Peg, he had his doubts. But he recognized those moments for what they were: the unavoidable echoes of strong feeling. He missed her, that was all. It was natural. He'd get over it.

He saw a Dairy King stand and realized he was hungry. He swung into the lot, went to the window, and got a chocolate cone with sprinkles. The April sun took some of the chill from the day, and it felt good to be out. He leaned against the car and ate the cone.

The afternoon was hectic at the office; every time he finished a call, another came in. By the time he'd initialed the contracts he'd gone home for, it was well after six and the place was empty. He straightened his desk, checked the contents of his briefcase, and checked again. He got his coat and went out.

It was the sprinkles that did it—three specks of chocolate on the seat of the Lincoln, where they'd been since lunch. He'd thought his coat was clean after he ate the ice cream, but apparently not.

He brushed them off the seat, cursing at himself. Just another example of how poorly he was operating.

He got into the car and closed the door. He put his key in the ignition. Then he did a strange thing.

He opened the door and stared at the sprinkles on the pavement. Something seemed to clutch at his heart; it felt as if it were being painfully squeezed. A sadness more acute than any he'd ever known swept through him.

"What the hell is this?" he asked aloud in the silent car. There were no answers, from without or within.

The night was terrible. He seemed to sleep only in half-hour stretches, and the awake times were all shadows and questions and memories. He dreamed a lot, haunting bits of his months with Peg and some nightmare scenes he couldn't decipher.

At four thirty he finally gave up. He showered and put coffee on. He could sense the decision taking shape, making itself, privy to resources his conscious mind hadn't caught up with yet. Instinct warned him not to rush it, not to brainstorm and ponder and bully the pieces into making sense, the way he did in real estate. This wasn't real estate—it was just *real*.

The sky was turning pink when he felt the first hint of peace, of an end to the turmoil that had plagued him these weeks. Slowly he saw: he'd been wrong. No, not just wrong; colossally wrong. A jerk. A rigid, defensive, unappreciative jerk.

He'd wondered all night about the sprinkles— why such a dumb thing had made him feel so rotten. Now he knew.

If he hadn't met Peg, he'd never have had to clean sprinkles out of his car. There wouldn't have been sprinkles *in* his car. Because he never in a thousand years would have done something as impulsive as stop for an ice cream and eat it in a parking lot, and let that be his lunch, and not think twice about it.

Working backward, he saw all the ways Peg had changed him—made him more open, happy, relaxed, able to enjoy life as he never had. How she had shown him, without saying a word—and undoubtedly without knowing she was doing it—that his respect for methods and rules and structure was overblown. That those things had their place, but not the exalted place they held with him.

He'd grown to love Peg for her free-spiritedness.

It sometimes got out of hand, but not in any way he couldn't accept. Not until the last thing—the night in the van when, thanks to her, they'd almost been killed.

He couldn't get past that. Dancing around a pool was fine, but her misjudgment with the thefts might have been tragic. Some of the night's chill crept back into his bones.

He got up and poured more coffee. The living room was fully light now, the morning sun warming it.

He went back again over everything that had happened in the van and before and after. It still infuriated him: he'd let her, at long last, talk him into helping her with the missing gowns, and look what had happened.

Yes? an inner voice challenged. What *did* happen?

We almost died, that's what, he answered. It was a fiasco.

Was it?

Of course. What else would you call it?

A success.

He leapt up, almost spilling his coffee. He was getting loonier by the minute; now he was having dialogues with himself. But it had shown him the answer.

And again, the key wasn't in the facts but in how he saw them. Peg's plan had been fine—a bit daredevilish for his taste, but basically sound. She'd done her research and groundwork, made tests, studied the details. Everything was in place; he'd never have cooperated otherwise. And in the end, it

185

had worked. She'd achieved her goal: the thieves were caught, the thefts stopped.

The flaw wasn't Peg's fault. She couldn't have foreseen that her friend would betray her. And it had been Peg's quick thinking and preparedness that had saved them.

But he hadn't been able to see that. Face it—he hadn't been willing. He'd chosen the David view, his typical tunnel-vision channel. Something went wrong, therefore Peg was wrong. If she'd played it *his* way, been as careful as *he* was, followed the rules, gone by the book. . . .

But if she'd done all that, the thieves wouldn't have been caught. And he wouldn't have had three of the most wonderful months of his life. And he sure wouldn't have become the kind of grown man who eats ice cream cones for lunch.

The peaceful feeling spread over him like a blanket. He looked at the phone near the couch. He wanted to call Peg; he longed to talk to her, share with her, ease away the hurt . . . to grab her and hold on, for good. But he knew that wouldn't be enough. Enough for Peg, maybe—his loving and forgiving Peg, who by rights should feel more rage than pain and probably didn't—but not enough for him, for *them*.

He had to find an approach that was a proper tribute to the warm, lively spirit that was Peg and all she did. A Peg way, not a David way. A way that symbolized his bottomless love and respect.

He poured still more coffee and settled back to plan.

* * *

"Women's Wear, Betty Henry speaking."

"Betty, this is David Robertson, Peg's friend."

"Oh, yes. How can I help you?"

"I need you to do me a favor. It may sound strange, but it involves a surprise for Peg, and I hope you'll help."

"Well, I . . . Well, of course, I suppose so."

"Wonderful. I'd like you to give Peg a message. Tell her—"

"Peg's in today. I'll get her."

"No, wait. The message isn't from me. That is, I don't want her to know I had anything to do with it. Tell her Detective Hirsh called—the one in charge of the thefts case. Say he wants her to meet him . . ."

"Hi, Mr. Robertson. Is being good afternoon, yes?"

"It sure is, Hassan. Listen—"

"You having day off?"

"I took the day off, yes. Now—"

"Mr. Robertson," Hassan said worriedly, "I never am knowing you to doing these things. You, how you saying? You setting clock?"

"What?" David asked.

"Clocks are setting by you, that's it. But no more."

"That's right, no more. I—"

"You are being in middle age now? What they call the male monopolies?"

David sighed. "No. Look, Hassan, I need your help."

The dark face went instantly serious. "Yes. Anything."

"First of all, did I get a delivery today? A box?"

"Yes. I am having in package room; I get it."

"Good, but first let me explain something quickly. Peg Bailey will be here soon—"

"Lady Bailey? I am not seeing her now for moch weeks. Is good—"

"Listen, there isn't much time. She's not coming to see me. I mean, she doesn't think she is. She expects to meet a detective here and check some evidence in Shirley Hewitt's apartment. So give her a key to twenty-two J and send her up."

"But only police are having key to twenty-two J."

"Hell," David said. "I'll just have to meet her at the apartment door, then. It won't be as good a surprise, but—"

"Excusing me?"

"Never mind. I'm talking to myself."

Hassan shook his head. "Mr. Robertson, you sure being weirdo, you don't mind saying me. You getting married or something?"

David gasped. "How did you know?"

The doorman's grin was huge. "Is being true?"

"I hope so," he said, reddening. "If she says yes." He checked his watch. "She'll be here any minute. Get my package, will you? And then I'll go to twenty-two J. Just send her up."

"Too late," Hassan said, nodding toward the door.

David saw Peg getting out of her car. She was beautiful, his sunny love. Her radiance shone through the heavy glass door. His heart swelled.

188

He stepped back into shadow.

"Hi, Hassan," she said as he opened the door.

"Lady Bailey! Or I should be saying"—he winked—"Lady Robertson?"

Peg's face filled with color. "What do you—David!"

"Hello, love," he said. He moved forward and gripped her hands. He wanted to do more, so much more, but he didn't dare yet. He wasn't a hundred percent sure she still wanted him.

"I love you," he said.

She looked dazed. "I'm—I'm supposed to meet—Do you? Do you really?"

"So much," he said. "I was an idiot. Can you ever—"

"You are forgiving," Hassan said. He was watching every move with fascination. He waved impatiently at David. "Ask her. Ask her for marrying."

Peg stared at Hassan. "What?"

"He's right," David said. "Annoying, but right. Please marry me."

Her eyes were wet. He saw happiness and hurt at war in her face. "But you—I thought—"

He bent and kissed her lips. "I'll explain it all. But please, make me happy—and give me the chance to make *you* really happy. Marry me."

"Oh, David. Of course." The tears spilled out.

"All *right!*" Hassan shouted. "I am now pronouncing—"

"Hassan, put a lid on it," David said. He took Peg in his arms. "You'll never be sorry, I promise. *I'm* sorry for a lot of things, but now that I know I have you—"

"You want package now?" Hassan asked.

David sighed. "Yes, please get the package. You spoiled my first surprise by proposing to Peg for me, but you can't spoil this one because you don't know what it is."

He took advantage of Hassan's absence to kiss her again. She responded eagerly, her wet face hot against his, her arms holding him close. Too soon, Hassan was back.

David took the big box from him and gave it to Peg. She pulled off the ribbon with shaking hands and raised the lid. Pushing the tissue aside, she lifted out the new Gatorade coat.

"It's exactly the same one," he said proudly. "I had to try four places before I found it. And we won't let any vacuum cleaners near it."

Peg closed her eyes briefly. She didn't know whether to cry again, or laugh, or both. She could see Hassan trying to keep a poker face.

"It's beautiful, David," she said. "Thank you." She put her arms around him and he hugged her as if he never wanted to stop.

"Don't you think it's beautiful, Hassan?" she asked, meeting his eyes over David's shoulder.

Hassan grinned. "Floor sure," he said.